HOLLY'S DILEMMA

After her aunt died, Holly learned that she had inherited her cottage in a rural part of Scotland. In her will, her aunt had said she hoped that Holly would follow her dream of becoming an artist and painting the beautiful Scottish scenery, but that if she didn't want to move to Scotland, her next door neighbour, Duncan McCall, should inherit the property. Holly had always loved her aunt's little cottage and was determined that no-one was going to chase her away — but she didn't know how difficult Duncan McCall could be . . .

Books by Eileen Knowles
in the Linford Romance Library:

THE ASTOR INHERITANCE
MISTRESS AT THE HALL
ALL FOR JOLIE

EILEEN KNOWLES

HOLLY'S DILEMMA

Complete and Unabridged

LINFORD
Leicester

First published in Great Britain by
Castle of Dreams
Darlington

First Linford Edition
published 1998

British Library CIP Data

Knowles, Eileen
   Holly's dilemma.—Large print ed.—
Linford romance library
1. Love stories
2. Large type books
I. Title
823.9'14 [F]

ISBN 0–7089–5311–5

Published by
F. A. Thorpe (Publishing) Ltd.
Anstey, Leicestershire
Set by Words & Graphics Ltd.
Anstey, Leicestershire
Printed and bound in Great Britain by
T. J. International Ltd., Padstow, Cornwall

This book is printed on acid-free paper

1

Arriving in Kirkston, the nearest town to Struan, Holly was fortunate in finding a parking place conveniently close to the solicitor's office. She would like to have had time for a coffee and to tidy herself up, but it was late morning and she didn't want to find he had gone to lunch, so she settled for putting a comb through her hair before hurrying to keep the appointment.

Looking at her reflection in the shop windows she wondered if perhaps the skirt she was wearing wasn't a little on the short side for such a noteworthy meeting; she seemed to be displaying a considerable amount of leg. Her short fair hair was already an unruly tangle of curls as she faced the wind blowing straight down the high street. The squally breeze brought colour to her cheeks as she strode quickly along the pavement, unwittingly attracting much attention.

She was an engaging twenty-two year old with a lively disposition, exuding health, vitality and love of life. Most people observed her as she passed them by, but Holly appeared to be totally oblivious to their attention — she wasn't at all pretentious about her appearance, merely smiling pleasantly at everyone she met in a friendly fashion.

On entering the solicitor's old fashioned building she gave her name to the rather cantankerous looking, elderly receptionist who requested her to take a seat while she found out if Mr Andrews was free. Holly looked about her with keen interest, pensively wondering if there would be any better prospects for work in Kirkston since so far she had drawn a blank in Prescot.

Looking again at the receptionist, she looked due for retirement she thought and giggled to herself, thinking that perhaps she went with the building. It was certainly very old, with little having changed over the years by the look of things — drab, dismal and colourless. She was wondering if all the inhabitants were of the same era, when somebody greeted her by name.

'Miss Davison. I'm Malcolm Andrews. Delighted to meet you at last.' The voice bellowed affably. 'May I offer you some coffee after your long journey?'

Mr Andrews was quite a surprise! He was youngish with a beaming round face and was decidedly tubby. He greeted Holly exuberantly, leading her into his office, pausing only to request coffee from the dour receptionist. His office was a mixture of magnificent old furniture and modern equipment, tastefully arranged for an oddly pleasing effect, not at all what she had expected from her glimpse of the rest of the building.

Holly found herself seated on a comfortable leather chair while he sat at the other side of the large oak desk in an executive swivel chair, his cherubic face beaming with delight. Crossing her legs decoratively. Holly carefully pulled at the hem of her skirt trying to cover her knees as Malcolm Andrews eyed her appreciatively.

'I'm very sorry about your aunt, but she died peacefully in her sleep, and she was quite old you know,' he said after a pause. Suddenly, he began rummaging amongst the various folders littering his desk before pouncing on one eagerly. 'I liked your aunt you know. She was a charming old lady and she never stopped talking about you, so I feel I know you already,' He grinned rather wickedly at Holly. 'She described you as being beautiful, talented and an efficient secretary — her very words. So where are you working at the moment?'

Holly realised that it must look odd her being able to come so quickly to see him. 'As a matter of fact I've been made redundant — along with half the work force at Bensons in Prescot,' Holly admitted ruefully. 'That is why I came straight away, in case I got a job interview later in the week and couldn't spare the time.'

'I'm very sorry to hear that. It's this recession — when will it ever end!' Mr Andrews sighed and picked up his paperwork again. 'Quite simply your aunt has left you the cottage — but there are strings attached. That is why I wanted to speak to you personally. It is a somewhat unusual arrangement which I will try to explain succinctly, then perhaps you will go to meet the next door neighbour. He can better fill you in with the details.'

Holly's immediate thought was how kind it was of her aunt to leave the cottage to her. She had always loved it and since her aunt didn't appear to have any other close relatives she wasn't doing anyone out of their inheritance. Then she frowned when she thought about the mention of a neighbour, Mr Andrew's tone held a note of caution.

'The last time I came to Struan the next door cottage was in the process of being renovated, but I never did meet the owner, he was away at the time. My aunt wrote and told me how helpful he had been to her though.'

'So you haven't met Duncan McCall? You have that treat in store.' Mr Andrews said with marked cynicism.

'Do I take it that he is a rather difficult individual?' asked Holly with surprise. From what her aunt had written in her letters he was absolutely wonderful; they got on like a house on fire — the perfect neighbour in fact. Every letter she received had mentioned him. Usually with a glowing reference about some deed he'd done for her. Holly surmised that he must be a middle-aged bachelor with plenty of spare time, and had been ingratiating himself on a lonely spinster.

'You might say that, although I haven't had much to do with the fellow. We don't handle his affairs. Your aunt however, thought the world of him — both solitary people I guess and found mutual comfort. Anyway, you will have to make up your own mind about him, suffice it to say that he isn't the sort of person one takes to immediately. Now, I must tell you the rest of the stipulations. Your aunt said that she hoped you would, with the help of a small amount of money she has left you, now consider following your dream. I hope that makes more sense to you than it does me!'

Holly's mind went back to a summer's day many years previously, when her aunt had asked her what she would really like to do if money was no object. She had replied instantly in a dreamy way that she would like to be a painter and try to capture the beauty of the Scottish scenery. Even at that tender age its grandeur impressed her. She had expected her aunt to scoff at such a wild idea but she hadn't, she'd merely said that one day she ought to try it perhaps.

Since then Holly had dabbled in her spare time, but hadn't taken it seriously enough to make it a full time occupation. The upkeep of the flat and car meant she had to have a permanent full time job, leaving little time for painting.

'Yes, I know what she meant,' she said quietly, reluctant to say more in case it made her look presumptuous. Mr Andrews looked a bit miffed at not being let in on her aspirations but she refused to be drawn.

'Since you have no job at the moment, do I take it that you will be coming to stay at the cottage?' the solicitor asked rather warily.

'Yes, I think I will.' Holly made up her mind instantly. It was a golden opportunity to do something different. She would love to live in Struan. In the past she had never wanted to return to Prescot at the end of her school holidays, and had pleaded with her aunt to let her stay. She had even asked why she couldn't go to the village school and stay there permanently, but her aunt had rebuked her for not thinking about what her parents would say to such a suggestion.

'I should tell you the rest of the story then,' said Malcolm Andrews leaning back in his chair thoughtfully, and making a pyramid with his hands as if in prayer. 'As I said, your aunt and Mr McCall got on famously so in the event of you not wanting to live there he has the run of the cottage — sort of like a caretaker. You couldn't sell it by the way, so if you didn't want to live there it would become Mr McCall's property anyway.' He looked at Holly thoughtfully weighing up his words.

'Look, in the circumstances I think the best thing would be for you to go and see the place for yourself, and to meet Mr McCall before making your final decision. You will have to be able to get along with him since he is the only close neighbour, and he isn't the easiest of people to deal with, as I mentioned.'

'I shall stay,' declared Holly in determined fashion. 'I have always loved my aunt's cottage so no next door neighbour is going to chase me away.'

Hazel eyes flashed with spirit. The very thought of being deliberately put off the cottage by a total stranger got her dander up. The cottage was part of her childhood and no interloper was going to take it over — especially when he already had a home of his own!

'I can see Mr McCall will have to watch out, Miss Davison. I hope you find everything in order. Please feel free to contact me at any time if you think I may be of assistance in any way at all.' Mr Andrews solicitously showed her out. 'You don't know yet what you are taking on,' he added rather ominously. 'Here's my card, ring me any time,' he repeated.

Holly went to find a small cafe for a light lunch before heading for Struan. After what Malcolm Andrews had said about her neighbour-to-be, she was ready to do battle if necessary, and one didn't do that on an empty stomach! Most of the time Holly got on well with people, she had a rather placid nature, but when roused by injustice she became a terrier, sticking to her guns in stubborn fashion.

During lunch she tried to envisage what it would be like living in Struan. When she'd stayed there as a child she had thoroughly enjoyed it, but that was when her aunt was alive — now it would be quite different. Would she be able to make a success of painting? Was it merely a pipe-dream? Was she chasing shadows?

Driving along the winding road by the loch, passed the small boatyard and the Old Bridge Hotel, the store-cum-post office and the church up on the hill, she felt she was coming home. Such a pleasant feeling of homeliness, serenity and calm. Everything looked the way it had always done. She smiled to herself as she drove passed the school, wondering what it would have been like to go there if her aunt had let her stay.

It was so wonderful to be back and the weak September sun greeted her benevolently, her only regret was that her aunt wouldn't be there to welcome her like before. She turned down the narrow lane leading to the grey stone cottage — one of a pair, and rumbled over the cattle grid before finally pulling on to the grass verge outside. It had been a long day already and she was feeling a little weary.

Her nerves jangled at the prospect of entering the empty cottage, so she paused to gaze around before walking down the short flagstone path to the front door. Looking to see what changes there had been since her last visit, she reviewed the renovations to the next door property. A charming porch extension, full of colourful plants, a new driveway and garage, all tidily done in keeping with the surroundings. She couldn't fault Mr McCall on those grounds — he obviously had some taste, despite what Malcolm Andrews had intimated!

Little looked different about her aunt's cottage though, except the paintwork was freshly done and the garden was neat and tidy — the michaelmas daisies tightly staked instead of flopping all over the path as before. That must be Mr McCall's doing too she thought, her aunt had never bothered in the past. He went up in her estimation and she wondered if perhaps Mr Andrews was in some way biased against Mr McCall — perhaps because he favoured others with his business maybe? I'd better wait and make up my own mind, she thought, and not jump to conclusions.

Extracting her overnight bag from the back seat she opened the small wooden gate — it still squeaked she noticed absentmindedly, as it had always done. Funny how little things brought back such fond memories. She walked down the short path to the front porch and as she inserted the key in the lock a furry bundle wrapped itself round her legs.

'Well now, Sooty, so you remember me do you? Come to welcome me have you?' She bent down to stroke the oversize black cat at her feet.

13

It purred noisily in recognition. 'You must be lost, poor old fellow without your mistress. Who's been looking after you? You're not exactly starving by the look of you.'

She let him into the cottage glad to have his company; the cat was at least something alive that she could take comfort in. Holly stood inside the front door taking stock before proceeding into the kitchen which was the place she remembered most acutely. It felt so dreadfully strange being there alone. She stared out of the window trying to hold back the tears or sorrow and recrimination. She wished with all her heart that she hadn't stayed away so long. Why hadn't she made the effort to visit her aunt more often? If only she had — but it was no use now. It was too late — two weeks too late. Her aunt was dead and the last time she had seen her was two years ago! Two whole years had gone by so quickly.

Pulling herself together she fed the cat that meowed incessantly since she'd let him in, then went for a tour of the cottage, noting the new night storage heaters with surprise. Her aunt had always derided any suggestion of change in the old fashioned heating arrangement — an open fire in the sitting room which heated the water too. Many a time, Holly recollected, she had shivered in her bed hugging a hot water bottle for comfort.

The cottage was pleasantly warm now, but that seemed to be the only alteration that she could see, apart from an extra door in the small hallway. It surprised her. She couldn't work out why it should be there, so she tried the handle cautiously. She knew that it must connect with the next building but curiosity had the better of her. An ear splitting noise erupted as soon as she opened the door and she jumped back in alarm, startled by the appalling cacophony. It was enough to waken the dead.

'What the devil is going on?' demanded the man storming through to shut off the alarm. 'Who on earth are you? No, don't tell me — you must be Miss Holly Davison I presume. Cassie's niece.'

'You presume correct. Now, can you tell me what is the meaning of this?' Holly shook her head trying to recover her equilibrium.

'You triggered the alarm. I suppose the dumb solicitor forgot to tell you about it.' A great bear of a man glared at her from his side of the doorway, he seemed so huge that he almost filled the available space.

'I meant why is there a door here in the first place? It wasn't there the last time I was here,' Holly snapped, instantly irritated by his bombastic attitude.

'It has been some time since your aunt had the pleasure of a visit from you,' the man growled impatiently. 'Cassie and I had an understanding. Look, you had better come through. We can't discuss things like this.'

Without waiting for her acceptance

he led the way into his sitting room, expecting her to follow meekly after him. Holly glowered indignantly but decided she had better go and get it over with — she had to make his acquaintance sometime.

She found herself being offered a seat while he perched nonchalantly on a chair arm opposite.

'I don't know much about you apart from what your aunt told me, and that I take with a punch of salt,' the stranger said scathingly. 'Your aunt made you out to be an absolute paragon and I have yet to find such a woman!'

The man was getting more insufferable by the minute. Holly bit back an angry retort as the man continued.

'Cassie and I had a perfect working relationship. I need peace and quiet for my work which she fully understood. Whenever I had to go out however, she would take messages for me, and occasionally she did a spot of tidying up and such like.

'For my part I kept an eye on her,

making sure that she was all right which is why we had the door put in to connect the two cottages. Cassie felt safer knowing I could help her at any time without breaking down doors. That is why it hasn't a lock, just the alarm on when necessary. Have you decided to live here?' he demanded, his black bushy eyebrows meeting in a deep scowl.

His abrupt, obnoxious manner stiffened Holly's resolve instantly. Even if she had been undecided before she now had her mind made up.

'Yes, I have,' she declared, squaring up to him somewhat belligerently. Today was proving to be an extremely difficult, tiring day indeed, now all she wished was some peace to come to terms with all that had happened. Major decisions were being taken hurriedly without due consideration, but she knew that she was going to stay despite this surly character in front of her. She could tell that he didn't look too pleased at the prospect and

18

that gave her a crumb of comfort.

'I hope you realise the conditions your aunt imposed,' he said, with somewhat intimidating ferocity.

Now she knew what Mr Andrews meant, he sounded absolutely impossible.

'I don't know much at all,' sighed Holly, her patience wearing thin. 'But it will have to wait until I have time to collect my thoughts. I've been up since six o'clock this morning, I'm travel weary, so if you'll excuse me I am going to go and make myself a cup of tea.'

She got up, smoothing her rumpled skirt and surreptitiously tugging it down a little as she noticed his eyes raking over her. She wished once again that she had put on a different outfit — something more elegant and suitable.

'You're wasting your time if you think that your undoubted feminine charm will make any difference to me,' he said smugly. 'Women are something I can get on very well without. In fact I have a definite preference for solitude.'

Holly pulled herself up to her full height — all five foot seven, and gave him a disparaging look.

'I might say the same about men,' she snapped waspishly.

He stood his ground looking distinctly menacing, his craggy face topped by a mop of dark wavy hair which he had ruffled absentmindedly as he talked. He could be a very attractive individual she thought, if only his manners and disposition were more pleasing.

He was much younger than she had anticipated — early thirties probably. He would make an interesting subject to paint sometime maybe — she could imagine he would look quite at home on the rugged hillsides. Mentally she visualised him playing the bagpipes with his kilt swirling as he strode through the heather; perhaps leading a regiment of men into battle even. Blinking at her own capricious thoughts, she realised she was letting her imagination get carried away.

'I'm sorry,' he said suddenly, completely taking the wind out of her sails. 'I'm having a bad day. Would you like some fresh milk? There isn't much food left in the fridge, so if you are short of anything give me a shout.'

She waited while he went to get the milk and as he opened the kitchen door a black and white collie dog hurtled out, barking excitedly.

'Down, Shep,' he ordered. 'You ought to be on your best behaviour making the acquaintance of the new neighbour.' Turning to Holly as he caught hold of the dog by its collar, he asked if she liked animals.

'Yes, I do. Is he friendly?'

'Usually — too much so I'm afraid. Not much good as a guard dog.'

While Mr McCall went back into the kitchen Holly made friends with the dog who was much more agreeable than its owner. It rushed to greet her, wagging its tail and offering her a paw

21

in affectionate fashion. Holly was down on her knees with Shep licking her face when the dog's owner came back into the room.

'I didn't mean that friendly, Shep. Down boy.'

'He's lovely,' Holly said, giving him a pat as she got to her feet. She took the proffered milk and thanked him.

'I'd better show you how to operate the alarm and then I will have to get on,' he said ushering her out. 'I'm expecting a call any moment.'

Holly found herself back in her aunt's cottage wondering what she was taking on. She sat at the kitchen table waiting for the kettle to boil, trying to decide if she was doing the right thing in even contemplating staying at the cottage. It felt strangely empty without her aunt's presence, but it was so familiar and homely that she knew, given half a chance she could be happy there.

Would she get that chance? That was the question. Having met Duncan McCall she now understood why

Malcolm Andrews had been cautious about her committing herself too soon. Duncan McCall was going to be quite a fly in the ointment! Why couldn't he have been a middle-aged or elderly bachelor instead of an attractive man with a bad temper?

I'm tired, she said to herself. What difference will it make having him for a neighbour? I'm quite capable of looking after myself. I don't need his help so perhaps our paths need hardly cross. She had lived on her own at the flat for four years now and hadn't needed assistance, so what difference would it make living at the cottage. Granted it was more isolated, but the village was only just down the lane. It wasn't as if it was miles from anywhere.

The cupboards and fridge were virtually bare as Mr McCall had predicted, so, determined not to call on her unfriendly neighbour for any assistance what-so-ever Holly decided to pay a visit to the village shop before it closed. Unearthing her flat walking shoes and anorak from the overnight bag she set off.

It felt wonderful to be striding out along the lane again, the clear fresh salty air coming in off the loch smelled sweet and invigorating. She breathed deeply to clear away the threatened headache brought on by the antagonism of her next door neighbour.

It was so good to be back in Struan. This was going to be her home now. She wasn't going to let him get to her. She was an independent spirit and had every right to live in peace in her aunt's cottage, so Duncan McCall would have to learn to live with it. So there, she said to herself. Once she had resolved that she impishly wondered, as she walked briskly along, what female had dared to upset the life of Duncan McCall! Obviously some woman had, she could tell from his hostile tone.

At the store she bought some bread and a few basic necessities, making friends again with the storekeeper whom she remembered from her younger days.

Nothing seemed to have changed in Struan for donkey's years as far as Holly could see. The very stability and continuity were quite reassuring, making her feel more than ever delighted to be able to stay and make her home there.

Back at the cottage she put a light to the fire already laid in the sitting room, and drew the curtains making it cosy and welcoming. Sooty took up residence on the hearthrug immediately and Holly sighed contentedly as she stretched out on the settee. A home of her very own and a chance to begin a new career maybe, what more could she ask — apart from a more agreeable neighbour?

She dozed for a while letting her thoughts wander over what she ought to do next. It was so tranquil — no traffic noise — no passers-by — the lane only continued past the cottages to a farm so was little used. All she heard were the natural country sounds of sheep and cows and occasionally a distant tractor, probably at the farm a mile down the lane, and the odd motor belonging to a boat out on the loch.

Her thoughts drifted on and she wondered what Duncan McCall did for a living. She didn't recall anyone saying — except that he needed peace and quiet. Well, as an artist that would suit her fine too! A little later she stretched and yawned, then went to make herself some tea which she had on a tray in front of the fire, tickling Sooty with her feet as he snoozed contentedly. Struan was a different world away from Prescot and she would find a way of earning her living there now she had the chance, neighbour or no neighbour!

It felt it was meant to be. It fitted in so well with being made redundant and not having found alternative work. Someone was telling her something. It was time to take stock of her life and do something different.

2

Sooty woke her early the next morning by pouncing on the bed, meowing loudly.

'Why don't you go and disturb Mr McCall,' Holly said yawning sleepily. 'I expect he's been looking after you recently hasn't he?' She turned over and tried to go back to sleep but the cat nuzzled up against her pleadingly, pawing at the covers rather impatiently.

'All right, all right, you win. I suppose I am your new owner. I can't think you'll get much sympathy from that ogre next door anyway. Whatever did aunt Cassie see in him?' she muttered wearily.

Crawling out of bed, she drew back the curtains and gazed out across the garden. Only a field separated it from the loch itself. It was such a scintillating autumnal scene to feast her eyes on,

27

making her so glad to be alive to enjoy it. The sun was peeping over the horizon, casting a golden glow on the bracken strewn hillside, and noisy seagulls whirled round a small fishing boat chugging up the loch. It was an artist's paradise. What more could one ask for she thought?

'Come on, Sooty old boy — breakfast.'

The cat immediately jumped from the bed and scuttled off with his tail waving in the air like a flag pole. Without bothering to get dressed Holly pottered downstairs in her night-gown to feed the cat. She hadn't packed a dressing gown but it hardly mattered as the place was pleasantly warm. In the kitchen she switched on the kettle to make herself a cup of coffee, and idly watched a seagull on the back lawn eating something — she knew not what. She was lost in thought so hadn't heard the door open, and it was only as she turned to get the milk out of the fridge that she became aware of Duncan McCall who had silently appeared in the doorway.

'Oh,' she squealed, realising how inadequately the night-gown covered her.

'Did I make you jump?' He smirked at her confusion.

'I didn't bring a dressing gown,' she gasped, blushing scarlet at her predicament.

'Well, don't let it bother you — it doesn't me. I told you, your feminine wiles leave me totally cold. Cassie didn't go around half naked though.' He seemed to be having difficulty in controlling his features as if holding back a chuckle. 'Trust me, you're safe enough in my presence. If it helps, think of me as your brother – a big brother who usually gets his own way that is.'

'I don't have a brother and I don't want a brother. Now what do you want?' Holly demanded angrily.

'I only came to feed the cat — something I have been doing for the past few days, and to ask if there was anything you needed. Also, to see if you were in a more receptive mood this morning. I gather that you are not, despite the welcoming sunshine. Ah well . . . '

'I've got everything I need, thank you very much.'

'Obviously,' he replied, looking her over from head to toe with great deliberation, his eyes glinting mischievously. 'I hoped you would be ready to agree terms, but maybe now is not an appropriate time. Prickly by nature as well as by name!' he observed cynically.

'Not usually but I'll make an exception in your case.' Holly moved to clutch the back of a chair shielding her lower half from his gaze and glared angrily back at him. 'I have decided to stay here, Mr McCall, whether you like it or not. I will have to return to Prescot to collect my possessions, and to pack up the flat, but then I'll be here to stay, permanently.' She emphasised permanently.

'Just like that! What about your job?' He quirked an expressive eyebrow.

'What job?' she snapped irritably. He seemed to be doing his best to undermine her confidence. 'I've recently been made redundant.'

'I'm sorry,' he said, grimacing ruefully and stroked his freshly shaved chin. 'I do seem to have the knack of saying the wrong thing to you, don't I? Well our talk can wait I guess until you return. There's no urgency.' He sauntered out of the kitchen calling 'Au revoir' over his shoulder, wafting the scent of his aftershave as he pulled the door to behind him.

Holly stayed where she was until she heard the click of the connecting door closing then let out a deep sigh, shuddering with animosity. Quickly she scurried up to her bedroom and threw on some clothes. He had definitely unnerved her despite his supposed apparent lack of interest in females. His sheer size was intimidating enough, but he radiated a domineering masculine confidence. A big brother indeed!

She frowned when she found herself thinking about him, wondering what it was that her aunt had found made him even passably likeable. True, he was arresting to look at with his dark, interesting features.

He was big and a well-made individual with broad muscular shoulders, yet with a surprisingly trim waist and hips which his tailored slacks stressed especially. He walked lightly despite his size, and his voice, when he wasn't snarling was a soft Scottish burr. She could well believe her aunt had felt comforted by his presence — he seemed so solid — so implacable. What a pity he had such a fiery temper.

Holly decided to go back to Prescot that day, stopping only to call on Mr Andrews to let him know that she was indeed going to live in Struan and that her neighbour hadn't put her off; in reality it was perhaps the very opposite. His aggressiveness was an added incentive on her part to stay.

However, the receptionist informed her that Mr Andrews would be engaged for some little time so Holly could only leave a message with her which she said she would duly pass on. She didn't look any happier this morning Holly noted, and she wondered if perhaps it was the surroundings that made her so doleful. That she could understand, the place looked so Dickensian.

Once on the road Holly concentrated on her driving trying not to let her mind wander too much on all that she had to do back in Prescot, although the change in her fortune excited her tremendously. Somehow, one way or another she would make a go of it for her aunt's sake as well as her own. She felt she had to because obviously her aunt Cassie had confidence in her ability and she didn't want to let her down. She smiled to herself at the thought of being a home owner and only twenty-two — whatever would her parents say!

During the next few days she packed

up all her belongings, fortunately she rented the flat fully furnished so she hadn't much in the way of large items to transport. On the Wednesday she visited her parents. They ran a hotel — one that opened all the year round which was why Holly had been sent to Struan so often as a child.

'Hello, Holly dear,' her mother greeted her, looking her usual harassed self. 'Have you managed to find another job yet?'

'No, Mum, and I'm not looking for one,' Holly said mysteriously.

That stopped her mother in her tracks. She looked puzzled and a little shocked. 'Why ever not, Holly? What are you going to live on? You could always come back here I suppose. We aren't full at the moment,' she added with a worried frown.

'Thanks all the same but I've come to tell you that I'm leaving Prescot,' Holly said breaking into a broad grin. 'I'm going to live at Struan.'

'Struan!' her mother looked askance.

'Cassie? Has anything happened to Cassie?'

'Yes, Mum. I'm sorry but I'm afraid aunt Cassie died three weeks ago and I have been informed that she left me the cottage in her will.'

'Oh dear,' said her mother, wiping her forehead with the back of her hand. 'I suppose she was getting on a bit, but it's still quite a shock. And you say she has left you the cottage, well that's nice for you dear. You always did seem to like the old place, I don't know why. It's so quiet, nothing ever happens there.'

'It's beautiful and peaceful,' Holly said with feeling. 'Anyway, I'm busy packing up my things and I am going back there on Saturday to live.'

'You had better go and tell your Dad. He was only asking yesterday if I'd heard from you — wondering how you were going to manage now you've left Benson's. He'll be sorry to hear about Cassie. I wonder why nobody informed us? We could have sent some flowers or something. What a shame nobody thought to tell us.' She went off muttering.

'Where is Dad?' Holly called after her as her mother disappeared down the rear stairs with her arms full of laundry.

'He's in the bar area trying to reorganise the tables I think.'

Holly went to find her father and tell him her news. She always felt on better terms with him, he seemed to at least understand her even if he hadn't the time to spare as often as he would have liked. She felt he would at least listen when she had something important to say or needed advice.

'What do you think, Dad? Do you think I should try my hand at being an artist? That is what Cassie wanted me to do.'

'Holly love, if you like living in that tiny cottage, it shouldn't cost the earth to run so what have you got to lose by having a go?' Her father poured her out a soft drink and she perched on a tall stool by the bar chatting while he finished drying glasses. 'You might be able to find work locally from time to time as a 'temp' to help eke out your savings. Kirkston isn't so far away is it from what I remember? It's been some time since we were last there, but I don't suppose it's changed much.

'You know that you can always count on us lass, but I say give it a shot while you're young and fancy free — if you really feel you'd like to that is. It's a golden opportunity and I look forward to attending your first exhibition. I don't know where you get your artistic talent from but it should be pursued.'

'Thanks, Dad,' said Holly glad to have his blessing. 'I feel it is what I would like to do and now is as good a time as any I guess. Jobs are definitely thin on the ground at present in Prescot. I haven't managed to even get an interview lined up.'

'That cottage is a little isolated you know, Holly. Are you sure that you will be all right there, especially during the long winter nights?' Her father looked at her anxiously. 'Is the next door property still vacant?'

'No. I have a neighbour,' Holly replied. 'I don't think I would like to have to call on him for anything except in an emergency though. He's a somewhat intimidating character, but aunt Cassie seemed to think the world of him apparently.'

'That's all right then. As long as there is someone there. You don't have to like neighbours, but it does help to make life more bearable, and if there was a real emergency you need someone to call on.'

Holly decided not to say any more about her new neighbour so quickly changed the subject by asking how they were managing during the recession which had hit every business in the town.

'We're holding our own,' her father said deliberately putting on a good front. 'We've a couple of conferences late on which help and we look as if we'll be fairly full for Christmas. Are you all right financially, Holly?'

'Sure. Aunt Cassie left me some money as well so I won't starve.'

'Don't forget to stock up with food for the Winter,' was her mother's parting shot as Holly kissed them both good-bye. 'Cassie used to get snowed in quite often I seem to remember.'

Holly's eyes sparkled at the prospect. 'I'll remember and get plenty of food in to last a siege,' she promised.

* * *

Saturday dawned cool and overcast but it couldn't dampen Holly's excitement. Today was the start of her new way of life. Today marked the beginning of her life as a painter. She had been to buy the requisite materials from the shop in Prescot, and they now resided in the boot of her car. The small car was almost full to overflowing with her possessions. She'd even had to leave some items with her parents for safe keeping, having accumulated more than she realised. At last with everything possible aboard she set off. Struan here I come!

It seemed such a momentous occasion that she wished she had someone to share her pleasure. She hadn't a boy friend at the moment and her cousin Roger was away on holiday so the only people to see her off were her neighbours from the flat below who were more than delighted to see her go. She had offended them one day by leaving the bath water to overflow while she answered the telephone. They had been most upset when the water cascaded down the walls of their newly decorated bathroom beneath, and hadn't accepted her profuse apologies. They hadn't spoken to her since.

It was a slow journey north, the car felt sluggish with all the luggage, but by mid-afternoon Holly was again turning down the lane to the cottage — *her* cottage! It had started to rain soon after leaving the motorway and it was now coming down in sheets. Hardly an auspicious start she thought as she ran quickly to the front door, almost falling over Sooty in the process who was lurking in the porch out of the rain.

When she got inside she decided that the unloading could wait until the worst had passed over and it was definitely time for something to eat. She hadn't stopped on the way except to have a thermos of coffee, and her stomach rumbled with hunger — it had been a long time since breakfast. She made one trip out to the car for the box of provisions containing the milk while the eggs and bacon were cooking. On her return she was startled to find Duncan McCall in the kitchen splashing fat over the eggs in the pan as if he owned the place.

'Welcome back,' he said, casually throwing her a towel to dry off her hair. 'Do you want a hand to unload?'

'No thanks,' she stammered, blinking with astonishment. 'I was going to leave it until the rain eases up.'

'That might be quite sometime,' he said casually taking time off to look out of the window, 'judging by the clouds up there. Still glad you came?' he mocked.

'It will take more than a drop of rain to put me off,' she snapped. All the time he had been finishing the cooking and deftly served it up on a plate.

'Come and eat it while it's hot.'

'I was under the impression this was my kitchen and I am more than capable of cooking myself a meal,' she said tartly.

'I was only being neighbourly,' he replied, pulling out a chair for her to sit down. 'The smell of the bacon cooking permeated to my nostrils so I came to see if I could help in any way. I'm sorry if we got off on the wrong foot the other day.'

He had the grace to look apologetic and by now Holly was mouth-wateringly hungry. 'I was having a bad day and the alarm going off was about the last straw.'

She took the offered seat and tackled the food with gusto trying to sort out her conflicting opinions. He appeared to be almost human today! Anyway he wasn't going to put her off her food — not when she was starving. While Holly ate her meal he made the tea, and uninvited sat down opposite her casually munching a piece of the toast.

'I don't believe I even introduced myself. I'm Duncan McCall as you have no doubt gathered. Pleased to make your acquaintance.' He grinned across as she finished the last bite.

'Holly Davison,' she said, shaking his hand rather incongruously. He looked different today — much more civilised and pleasant, almost rakish she thought. 'It's great to be back, and for your information. I also like peace so I'm quite sure that you will hardly know that I am around.'

'I was like a bear with a sore head last

Monday wasn't I?' he smiled ruefully. 'Due to discovering that I had been working all weekend for nothing. The client suddenly changed his mind and all my work was useless.' He leaned back, balancing his chair on two legs rather precariously.

'Exactly what sort of work do you do?' Holly asked, feeling a little more sociable now that she had eaten and the ogre was looking much more congenial.

'I trained as an engineer, but now I do mainly design work — computerised drawings for the engineering business, and some computer programming. Didn't your good friend the solicitor tell you?' he asked arching his eyebrows enquiringly. 'That is a surprise!'

'Mr Andrews didn't tell me much at all,' she said, nibbling her lower lip, thinking about what the solicitor had said. 'He was leaving it to you to explain. I gather that my aunt has left me the cottage but with strings attached. I'd like to know what those *strings* are.'

'I suppose now is as good a time as any,' he said pouring them both some more tea, obviously quite at home in Cassie's kitchen. 'Cassie was a dear old soul. I liked her. We got on famously. Over the last eighteen months she had gradually been failing, so I tried to make her life as comfortable as possible. I managed to persuade her that she needed more heat about the place, so when I installed the heating in my cottage I put some in here as well. She, being an independent old lady wanted to repay in some small way, so I let her do some housework. She would cook the odd meal, darn my socks — that sort of thing, making her still feel wanted.'

He had genuinely liked her aunt she could tell by the tone of his voice when he spoke of her. His voice was soft, almost velvety when he spoke of Cassie. Holly could well understand her aunt would want to do something in return for his kindness, and she warmed to him for his thoughtfulness in dealing with what could have been an awkward situation.

'Well, as you can see, I am quite capable of looking after myself, so I'm sure that once I get installed you will hardly know that I'm around,' she said quietly but firmly. He had brought back the guilty feeling she had of not being there when her aunt needed her.

'When Cassie told me what she intended to do about the cottage I tried to dissuade her.' Duncan went on, frowning as he toyed with a teaspoon. 'I didn't think any young woman in their right mind would want to live in such an out of the way place. I did my best to put her off but she was most insistent that you would probably jump at the chance, as you obviously have.'

'Mr McCall. I spent many happy holidays here in my youth and now that I have the opportunity to follow my dreams I intend to do that. Cassie knew what I have always wanted to do and I intend to make a success of it for her sake as well as my own,' Holly said somewhat forcefully.

'I know, I know, keep your hair on. I do understand. Cassie did explain everything to me, but I had never met you. I hadn't anything to go on. Anyway, she told me that you were a trained secretary and would help me out with my correspondence, but I don't suppose Mr Andrews told you that either.'

Holly opened her mouth to speak but he launched his next salvo. 'In the event of you not wanting to stay, the cottage was to become an extension of mine. I promised Cassie that I would always look after it. If you opted to stay, she said no doubt we would help each other out. She held you in very high regard I might add, and was anxious about you living here alone. I promised I'd look out for you and keep the wolves at bay, although from the look of you, you are hardly out of the cradle.'

'What sort of assistance had you in

mind Mr McCall?' Holly asked, when she finally managed to get a word in. His tone had changed, he sounded scornful of her aunt's impression of her niece's capabilities. Holly's hackles rose. She knew she looked young for her age, especially dressed as she was now in jeans and sweat shirt but she was annoyed by his insensitivity.

'Do you think you could start by calling me Duncan?' he smiled disarmingly. 'As I said, I believe, I am quite self-sufficient but occasionally when I have to go away on business it would be helpful if you could take messages for me. Also, since you are a trained secretary, I would certainly value your assistance with my correspondence and such-like. Nothing too onerous!' he declared.

'Look, I am here to stay,' Holly said tightly, not over happy at the stress he placed on the words *trained secretary*. He had summed her up as a child with a doting aunt she could tell, and he had no real confidence in her capability. 'I am quite willing to fulfil my aunt's wishes to the best of my ability, but I am going to work hard at my painting so I don't know when I will be available for secretarial duties.'

'Shall we see how it goes,' he said softly. 'I know we got off on the wrong foot to start with, but I'm not usually so intolerant — at least for most of the time I think. Last Monday wasn't one of my better days.'

Holly could only nod her head in agreement, she didn't wish to antagonise him too much, but she wasn't going to be at his beck and call too readily. He was too arrogant by half.

'Just to show how wrong I can be sometimes, it looks as if the rain has eased off, so can I give you a hand unload your car now?' he said, glancing through the window as he got to his feet.

It didn't take them long to pile her belongings in the hall and sitting room.

'Well, I should get back to work. Thanks for the tea. Give me a shout if there is anything you need a hand with,' he said in a neighbourly way. 'I'm glad you decided to stay, Holly Davison. I guess Cassie was right after all.'

He had gone before she recovered from the shock statement. She flopped down on the stairs in bewilderment. After the way Malcolm Andrews had described Duncan McCall she had been expecting the worst, but the man she had been talking to didn't bear any resemblance to the monster she met last Monday.

He would take some getting used to after her last employer who had been very easy going, but as for doing some secretarial work, well that shouldn't prove to be any hardship surely. It could hardly amount to such a big deal — not after her experience at Bensons. She set about unpacking with some enthusiasm.

3

During the next few days Holly settled into her new regime and didn't see anything of Duncan at all. At first, she smiled to herself when she thought how anxious she had been about continually crossing swords with him, but it was so quiet that she never really knew when he was in or not. The only time she saw him was when he took the dog for a walk.

After a while she grew annoyed with herself for actually wanting to see him, wanting him to call on her. When he didn't she felt frustrated. Solitude was all very well but taken to extremes it was unsettling, especially as until recently she'd been used to a busy office life. She would have welcomed some company, even his, and would have been happy to do some work for him.

Every time she passed the hall door she wondered what she ought to do about it. Since he had walked into her kitchen on that first morning she had remembered to be decently clothed in case he appeared again unannounced. It began to look as if it was an isolated occasion. He gave the impression of being totally disinterested in her as a woman, so she had nothing to worry about on that score, but his scornful remarks still stung about her looking so young. Maybe it was best to leave it as aunt Cassie had it, and treat him like a big brother as he suggested.

She missed the camaraderie of the works and the sense of urgency and importance which her job had provided. After six years at Bensons she missed it badly, although she was trying to adapt to her new way of living. She used to enjoy being at Struan, but it had been so different when her aunt was alive. Now it felt too quiet — far too quiet, and it was taking some getting used to. It seemed strange not to see another soul from one day to the next unless she made the effort to go to the village, or the postman called. She was certainly glad to have Sooty for company.

The following Friday it was raining again. She couldn't go out sketching so she decided to do some baking instead. Cassie had taught her to bake and soon she was busy like the old days. A small freezer in the pantry was a new acquisition — another of Duncan's suggestions no doubt! She began to wonder what her obligations to Duncan were. She couldn't bring herself to ask but she knew that she was in his debt for all that he had done over the past two years when she hadn't even visited. She felt so guilty about that. After all her aunt had done for her over the years, when she needed some assistance herself Holly hadn't been there, and it rankled that it had been left to a stranger to look out for her.

Suddenly it came to her that she could at least provide Duncan with some good old-fashioned home cooking — she doubted if he did more than cook easy meals or heat up ready prepared frozen ones. Pleased that she had an excuse to go next door she made up a batch of buns, scones and a meat pie, and carefully disengaged the alarm before going through the connecting door. She had never been in his kitchen and as she crossed the bottom of the stairs she could hear his muffled voice on the telephone somewhere upstairs. The kitchen was quite a revelation — all modern units with oak doors, still keeping the cottagey atmosphere. It was beautifully spruce and tidy as if to bear out her theory.

She placed her baking on the table and left quietly, not wanting to disturb him whilst he was obviously busy. He must have converted one of the bedrooms into an office she thought, wondering what the rest of the house was like. She remembered the lounge vaguely from her last visit but she had been too uptight to take particular notice of its furnishings. She had a blurred recollection of autumnal shades, and it being warm and cosy. He certainly had a comfortable existence if one liked solitude, she reflected — it was much more cosy that her own.

She cleared away her baking and washed up in time for lunch, wondering if he would take a break and come to thank her, but he didn't. She mooched about for a while waiting but still he didn't come. Eventually, feeling a slightly piqued, she put on her outdoor clothing and went for a walk by the loch. She couldn't understand what was wrong with her. She wanted to see him again for no good reason, there was nothing she needed. She looked about for inspiration for her painting but she wasn't in the mood. She felt thoroughly depressed.

She was cross when she returned to the cottage to see that he had called whilst she was out and left her a note of thanks propped up on the kitchen table. That made her all the more despondent, the thought that she had missed him after all. Mentally she kicked herself when she remembered how she had told him that she liked her solitude, and she wouldn't be seeing much of him once she started painting. Too much solitude — that's the problem she muttered to herself angrily, I'm not used to it.

By the following Tuesday she was ready to go and ask if there was anything she could do for him when suddenly he appeared, like the proverbial Cheshire cat. She hardly recognised him dressed in his smart city business suit. He carried a bulging brief case and some rolled up drawings.

'Hi,' he said brightly. 'I've got to go out. Do you think you can take messages for me?' He held out a portable phone.

'I guess so,' she said calmly, trying not to look over enthusiastic. 'I don't have any plans to go anywhere today.'

'Thanks. I not sure how long I'll be. I have to go to Glasgow.'

'Are you taking Shep?'

'No. I'll leave him in the back garden, if that's all right by you. He's not awfully keen on cities any more than I am.'

'Have a safe journey.' She said it automatically, forgetting that she wasn't at Benson's and he wasn't her old boss.

'Thanks, I'll try.' He breezed out, obviously eager to be on his way.

Holly stood watching at the sitting room window as he got his car out and motored off towards the village, thinking how confident and reassuring he was to have as a neighbour. Knowing he was next door made her feel safe. She would feel extremely lonely and vulnerable by herself she realised, and wondered how her aunt had managed all those years when the cottage next door had been empty much of the time.

Feeling a little curious about Duncan McCall's cottage, now seemed a good time to have a peek while he was away.

She went through the communicating door carrying the phone, feeling a little apprehensive, rather like an intruder. She could hear clicks and whirrs coming from what should be the front bedroom and went to investigate. Gingerly she pushed open the door, and was confronted by an elaborate array of computer equipment and electronic gadgets. It all looked highly technical and impressive.

Not daring to touch anything she hastily closed the door and went into the back room which was obviously his bedroom. She smiled when she saw some of her aunt's feminine touches — a pot plant on the window sill and little crocheted mats dotted about. She straightened his hair brushes, picked up a paperback off the floor and hung his dressing gown on the hook on the door. No photographs on the dressing table she noticed, or even pictures on the walls. Maybe she could rectify that omission she thought.

A large double bed dominated the

room, but with the alcoves converted into fitted wardrobes there was still plenty of floor space. Straightening the bedcovers she found herself blushing at the way her thoughts were wandering to its owner, thinking he would need a big bed to accommodate his large frame. Then quickly she left the room in case he returned unexpectedly, anxious not to be found snooping there of all places!

In the bathroom the smell of his tangy aftershave still lingered, she sniffed appreciatively and in passing noticed the overflowing linen basket. Before she knew what she was doing she had taken the dirty washing downstairs and put the first load in the machine. Whilst that was getting done she started on the hoovering and dusting, as her aunt must have done previously. At least it would be some recompense for his kindness to her aunt she thought, she could hardly offer him money.

The ringing of the 'phone startled her making her nearly drop the ornament she was dusting. She answered it rather uncertainly.

'Where's Duncan?' the woman's voice crackled harshly.

'I'm afraid he's away today. Can I take a message?' Holly asked politely.

'Who might you be?' the woman asked shrilly, sounding more than a little perturbed.

Holly smiled to herself and mischievously said, 'I'm his cleaning lady. How may I help you?' She heard the receiver being slammed down at the other end and wondered wryly if she had upset Mr McCall's love life. Musing as to who the woman could have been she continued with the housework, trying to decide if she should mention her to Duncan when he returned, but since she had no name of the caller it seemed irrelevant. If it was a girl friend no doubt he would hear about it soon enough!

By teatime she had cleaned the house from top to bottom and there was a neat pile of ironing all done. There had been two other telephone calls during the afternoon about office matters. She made notes of the messages leaving them next to the ironing, and a casserole simmered gently in the oven. She took a last look round before returning to her own cottage to prepare herself a meal.

She was sitting with her feet up watching television feeling very virtuous when she saw the lights of his car returning. Smiling happily to herself she was thinking how surprised he was going to be, and expecting him to come to thank her for all her hard work. She had enjoyed doing his housework and looked forward to him showing his appreciation. She waited and waited but still he didn't come, until eventually, feeling a little aggrieved, she decided to take him back the phone and to see if he was all right.

'You have been a busy bee,' he snapped when she found him in the kitchen. He'd removed his jacket, loosened his tie and was sitting at the table reading through the messages and post that had arrived after he left that morning. He hardly glanced in her direction as he scowled at the letter in his hand.

Holly was quite taken aback. Here she was expecting gratitude for her hard work on his behalf and all he did was snarl at her.

'If you've moved anything in my office I'll murder you. Curiosity got the better of you did it?'

Her cheeks flamed, realising how accurate the description was.

'You said aunt Cassie used to do your housework so I thought . . . ' She couldn't continue, throwing the phone on the table she turned and ran from the room, her face was red with anger and embarrassment.

Back in her own cottage she hurled herself down on the settee. The ungrateful moron! Well, that was the last time she would ever do anything for him she told herself. She would get a bolt fitted to that door and shut him out of her house for good. She never wanted to see him again. Never! Never! Never! She thumped the cushions angrily.

A little while later she dragged herself upstairs to soak in the bath then, wrapped in a towelling dressing gown she made herself a hot drink, all the time cursing the very day she had set eyes on Duncan McCall. Mr Andrews had been right after all, the man was impossible!

She slept badly. She was beginning to wonder if it was all a mistake. Maybe she wasn't cut out for life in such rural surroundings. She should have stayed in Prescot and looked for another secretarial post. It had been different when aunt Cassie was alive. Struan had been such a pleasant, happy place to stay.

The next day Holly was up early to go into Kirkston to do some very necessary shopping — anything to get as far away from Duncan McCall as possible. During the night she had resolved to stay at the cottage and continue with her plan. Why should she be chased away from Struan by one domineering male! He had spoiled what had been an amicable arrangement by his churlish behaviour but she could surely ignore him. Apparently he thought it was all right for him to wander into her cottage whenever he felt like it but it didn't work the other way round. Well, we'll see about that!

Her first port of call in Kirkston was the hardware store where she bought a bolt and a screw driver. As she walked along the high street towards the supermarket she met Mr Andrews, who hailed her cheerily.

'This must be my lucky day,' he beamed. 'Can I tempt you into joining me for coffee? You look as if you could do with one. I've been wondering how you were getting on with you-know-who.'

Holly was feeling so dispirited that she accepted Mr Andrews suggestion with pleasure. He took her by the arm and led her into Kirkston's finest restaurant, chatting casually until their coffee arrived.

'Now then, Holly — may I call you Holly?'

'Please do,' she said, it was nice to see a friendly face after the conflict with Duncan.

'You must call me Malcolm.' He stretched across the table and took her hand in his, taking her by surprise. It seemed such an affectionate thing to do when she hardly knew him. 'How are you getting on with your neighbour, Holly? Have you come to some sort of workable arrangement? I've been bothered about you.

'If you had asked me that the day before yesterday I would have said everything is fine and dandy,' she replied with a sigh, 'but now, well . . . ' She removed her hand slowly from his grasp.

'Why? What's happened?'

'Yesterday, Mr McCall had to go to Glasgow so he asked me to take 'phone messages,' Holly said, relieved to have someone to talk to and get it off her chest. She wasn't over-enamoured with Malcolm Andrews but at least he was prepared to listen. 'Since I wasn't going anywhere I did some housework for him, thinking it would in some small way pay him for his kindness to my aunt. I cleaned the cottage from top to bottom, did a stack of washing and ironing and left him a casserole for his supper.'

'I say, that was mighty decent of you, old girl. He should have been mighty grateful.'

'Apparently, Mr Duncan McCall thought differently! He accused me of snooping — the ungrateful moron!'

'He did what? The despicable fellow! How contemptible! After you worked your fingers to bone for him. I never liked the man! Whatever your aunt saw in him I'll never know.'

'He can be quite charming on occasions,' Holly said, unexpectedly leaping to Duncan's defence.

'So, what are you going to do now?'

Malcolm asked. 'It will make it jolly awkward living next to someone you can't stand won't it?'

'He's not going to force me out of my aunt's cottage so easily. I've been to buy a bolt to put on that connecting door so I'll not have him walking in so freely in future.' She beat her hand on the table making the crockery rattle alarmingly. 'I'll show him that I'm no pushover.'

'Good for you, Holly. I don't know what arrangement he made with your aunt but it wasn't in writing so far as I know so you've nothing to worry about on that score.'

'Do you know who paid for the new heaters around the house, and the freezer in the pantry? I feel as if I am beholden to him, because maybe he purchased various things for my aunt latterly to make her life comfortable.'

Malcolm shook his head. 'Whatever he did for Miss May has nothing to do with you, Holly. You have no need to reimburse him in anyway. I think you are very brave to stay at the cottage. It's so isolated.' He shuddered theatrically.

'Oh, I love the cottage,' said Holly, her eyes alive with pleasurable remembrances. 'I always have. I don't think of it as being isolated when the village is only just down the lane.' She wished she had a pleasant neighbour that's all, that would make all the difference.

'You wait until the winter sets in, the lane might seem a lot longer then!' Malcolm said pulling a face. 'You might think differently when you're snowed in for weeks on end with only that boor of a man next door. Anyway, I hope that you will stay, and we must do this more often. I enjoy taking charming young ladies out for coffee.'

'And what would your wife think?' Holly asked shrewdly. It was a shot in the dark that he was married, and when she saw his face growing red she knew she had been correct.

'Mhairi wouldn't mind — after all,

you are one of my clients,' he blustered. 'I like to keep my customers happy. All part of the service we provide.'

Holly made a mental note to be cautious about accepting invitations so readily in future, she didn't want to be the cause of any notoriety. She knew how rumours spread like wildfire in the area and she didn't want to get that sort of reputation.

After lunching in town, with the weather closing in, she decided to return home. For the first time that she could remember she approached the cottage with mixed feelings. She had spoken heatedly to Malcolm about staying but now she wasn't too sure.

On the kitchen table she found a note of thanks for the casserole and a brief apology. Holly read it through, then crossly tore it to bits. He needn't think he can placate me so easily, she muttered as she unwrapped the new bolt. I'll show him that he can't take me for granted. He thinks I'm a mere child does he!

Fitting the bolt proved to be much more difficult than she had imagined but finally she managed to tighten the last screw and sat back with delight when the bolt shot home. She locked the front and back doors and for the first time since she had arrived the cottage felt completely hers. No intruders could get in, and that especially meant Mr Duncan McCall!

She wondered how long it would be before he discovered the new development and grinned to herself when she thought how it would displease him. For the rest of that day she kept one ear listening for him trying the door but nothing happened, much to her intense irritation. She was rather relishing the confrontation.

* * *

The next day turned out bright and sunny. Holly bounced out of bed determined to accomplish something. Blow Duncan McCall, she had work to do. Time she got on with her painting and stop messing about, she berated herself. She should stop moaning about Bensons and everything else in Prescot. Struan was now her home. It was a new way of life and she had better get used to the idea. She didn't need neighbours, especially bad tempered boorish ones. She could be self sufficient if she tried, like her aunt Cassie had been all those years.

After breakfast she packed her sketching gear along with a few sandwiches in a rucksack, then set off along the path opposite the cottages that would take her up the hillside. She hoped to get a view of the loch from higher up with the yachts at anchor, it should make a picturesque scene. She felt the urge to prove herself. Today she wanted to forget Duncan McCall and make a good start on her new career. She knew that the days when she would be able to get outside would be limited now so she wanted to make the most of it, while she was in the right frame of mind too.

She found a vantage point from which she could view the valley right down the loch to the estuary. Then, perched on a large boulder she surveyed the scene with a deep sigh of satisfaction. She felt her animosity towards Duncan McCall dissipate as she let the beauty of her surroundings permeate her mind. It was a glorious day — a day when one couldn't help being at peace with the whole world. It was intoxicatingly clear, she could even see on the rocky shore some distance away what she thought were seals romping in the shallows.

Soon, completely absorbed in her work she sketched with light, quick strokes in a world of her own, totally oblivious of anyone or anything but the scene in front of her. She had put Duncan McCall out of her mind.

As she watched the activity down in the boatyard her attention was drawn to a magnificent motor launch edging up the far bank. Someone must be extremely wealthy to possess that she mused as it disappeared from her sight round a small headland. Not the usual craft for these waters.

How long he had been standing there she didn't know but suddenly Holly became aware that she was no longer alone. Then Shep nosed up to her before being sharply reprimanded by his owner.

'I didn't mean to distract you,' Duncan said as he drew closer, his voice was a soft burr again.

'Out of all the valley why did you have to come here to annoy me?' she demanded angrily.

'Because I want to apologise.'

'So, you've apologised. I got your note.' She glared at him, wishing he would go and leave her in peace.

'Holly, please forgive me. I know I behaved badly. I realise that you probably only wanted to help.' He was now only an arm's length away, his body completely blotting out the view she was sketching, his eyes on a level with hers.

'I've told you, I accept your apology. Now please go and let me get on with my work.' Holly stared back down the track not wanting to look into his face. She didn't like being at odds with anyone but he was really something else. She had never met anyone so brusque as him before.

'Why did you put the bolt on the door?'

'Because I want my privacy as much as you apparently want yours,' she snapped. 'I have no wish to have a repetition of Tuesday so in future I will keep myself to myself and hope you will do the same.'

Duncan ran his hands through his hair in a distracted way, he paused before replying. 'I know you have every right to be angry with me. It wasn't your fault — I was in a bad mood. It's something that happened sometime ago and you bore the brunt of my irritation.'

'Whatever it is that gets into you I don't know or care. Just leave me alone,' Holly said despondently. 'As far as I know all I have done is what any neighbour would have done — like Cassie did no doubt, but obviously you don't see it like that, so let's forget it shall we? You go your way and I'll go mine then hopefully we shan't see much of each other.'

'Oh, Holly, you're not a bit like Cassie,' he said with a deep sigh. 'She was old and fragile, it was easy to accept her tokens of assistance. You are quite different. You have a disturbing effect on me. Something I vowed would never happen again.'

'I'm sorry, I can't alter my appearance for you,' she said through gritted teeth.

'I wouldn't want to change you one little bit,' he replied with a winning smile. 'You are beautiful — stunningly so. That's part of the problem.'

Holly turned to stare at him. 'You said that women had no effect on you if I remember.'

'That was before — before you came into my life, Holly.'

Eyes dark as midnight stared back at her, she could feel herself drawn to them like a hypnotised rabbit. He looked so captivatingly handsome in a wildly rugged sort of way.

She shook her head in disbelief at her fickle thoughts and looked away, trying to regain her equilibrium. She'd heard of men having charisma, well he certainly had it, whatever it was. She felt as if she had no willpower to stay angry with him for long and she could feel herself relenting.

'I take it that you don't have a high regard for women in general,' she sneered.

'No, I'm afraid I haven't. When one has been badly let down as I have it makes one careful about repeating the experience.'

'Yes, I know from recent first-hand experience!' She saw that her barb had hit home.

'Holly, please can we make a fresh

start? I will try to control my temper. I need to make my peace with you so that I can get on with my work. I haven't done anything constructive since Tuesday night.' He sounded desperate.

'As far as I am concerned the episode is over and done with,' she replied, trying to control her irrational feelings. 'I am hoping to get on with my life and not be reliant on anyone. What I did, I did because I thought I needed to in some way repay you for what you did for aunt Cassie. The heaters and the freezer must have made her life much more comfortable. I only wish I had been to see her more often and done things for her rather than leave it to a stranger.'

'You shouldn't reproach yourself. Cassie understood. I was only being neighbourly.' He smiled wryly realising what he had said. 'May I take you out to dinner to make my peace with you? Please? I'm not much of a cook myself but I owe you a meal. We could go over to the King's Arms at Lawton.'

Holly couldn't resist the pleading look. His eyes softened to a deep honey, his voice was stirringly persuasive.

'All right,' she conceded. 'A peace offering.'

'Great. I'll call for you at seven. OK?' With a reminder not to catch her death of cold he strode off down the hill whistling for Shep who was chasing about in the bracken.

Holly watched him go until he disappeared out of sight round the bend in the track then pulled out her sandwiches and thermos. The mood had changed and she needed time to recapture it if it was possible, which she very much doubted. What was it about the man that she found herself always accepting his apologies so readily? Surely she wasn't reduced to accepting any invitation simply for the need for some company! Why on earth had she agreed to go out to dinner with him? She couldn't believe that she had accepted his request so readily.

She sighed and doodled while she ate the rest of her lunch. It was only as she was screwing up the paper bag that she noticed what she had drawn. It was quite a good likeness of Duncan she thought as she touched it up a bit. She didn't think he would care for it though. She had drawn him scowling, his dark eyebrows a deep vee, his eyes partly hooded as he looked into the sun were hard and piercing, his mouth tight and stern.

She stayed for a little longer without achieving anything worthwhile. The interruption had unsettled her concentration so she packed up her gear and returned to the cottage by a circuitous route. By the time she got back she felt quite excited at the prospect of the evening ahead and spent a long time soaking in a herbal bath, mulling over what to wear for her date. She got to wondering again who the woman was who had let him down and what she had done to cause his wrath.

4

Pulling out a pale blue dress made of fine wool Holly slipped in over her head and stood back to admire herself in the wardrobe mirror with a nod of satisfaction. It suited her she thought, with its scooped neckline and long sleeves — demure but attractive. It was one of her favourites with a fitted waistline and short flared skirt showing off her trim waist and shapely legs to their best advantage. You'll do she said to herself, as she brushed her hair into a halo of curls to frame her face, pleased that she'd had time to wash it on her return. She had no idea what sort of place the King's Arms was but she felt dressed appropriately for any occasion.

A few minutes before seven Duncan knocked on the communicating door. She hadn't anticipated him coming that way so she hurried to unbolt it. His eyebrows shot up and he whistled through his teeth.

'Wow!' he said. 'Such a sight will have all the young men for miles around knocking at your door. I may have more trouble than I bargained for when I promised Cassie I'd watch out for you.'

Holly bit her lip apprehensively. 'Am I over dressed do you think? I can go and change, it won't take me long.'

'Oh no you don't. You look terrific. I shall be the envy of every hot blooded male around that's all. You're quite an enigma, young Holly. At times you look like a gangling teenager needing protection, and then you appear like now — absolutely incredible. You could have men eating out of the palm of your hand merely to be seen with you I suspect.'

His charming observation made her blush. 'Well, for your information I am twenty-two years old — no longer a teenager and I'm starving.'

He grinned and helped her on with her coat. 'Come on then. Let's go eat. I must admit to quite a healthy appetite myself. Glad to hear you're not one of those lettuce leaf fanatics.'

It proved to be a wonderful evening. Duncan was obviously on his best behaviour and kept her charmingly entertained. The King's Arms was a pleasant up-market hotel so she was pleased that she felt suitably dressed. She glanced across the table at Duncan. In his dark suit and white silk shirt he looked extremely distinguished, and he smiled back reassuringly.

'Penny for your thoughts,' he said softly.

'I was thinking that I don't know anything about you apart from your name, that you are an engineer and you have a penchant for helping elderly old ladies.'

'What would you like to know?' His eyes twinkling impishly in the subdued lighting.

'Everything. Where you were brought

up, have you any family and what brought you to Struan?'

'That's quite a tall order. Thirty two years to be condensed into a few minutes,' he said archly.

So he was thirty-two. 'I'm not in any hurry,' she said demurely. 'We have all evening haven't we?'

'OK, I guess you should know something about the *brother* you inherited along with the cottage.' He grinned teasingly. 'I grew up in Oban. My parents owned a shop — a newsagent which kept them pretty busy. Long opening hours, seven days a week, etc., although on Sunday not all day. I was an only child so I became used to spending long periods on my own as you will no doubt appreciate.'

'Same here, only my folks are hoteliers,' she said with sympathetic understanding.

'When I left school I went to university were I trained to be an engineer. I obtained my degree and got a job down in the Midlands for a while feeling rather like a fish out of water. I enjoyed the work but hated living down there; it was so far removed from what I was used to.

'Then five years ago I came back to Scotland when my mother became terminally ill. I helped my father with the business and started doing freelance work using the computer that I'd bought for a hobby. A year later when my mother died my father sold the business leaving me free to concentrate on my career again full time.'

The conversation was momentarily interrupted by the arrival of their first course.

'I took a flat in Oban and gradually built up my work load, doing mainly computer programming. One day, I met another computer buff called Alec. Together, Alec and I worked on a project which we thought was going to make us our fortunes. It's too complicated for me to explain in detail but it was simple yet ingenious and

we worked long hours refining it.'
Duncan's face grew solemn; a far away
look came into his eyes and his voice
hardened perceptively.

Holly wondered what was coming
next, he looked so — so angry.

'Alec had a sister called Alison,' he
went on in a cold, icy tone. 'I started
going out with her — my first real
romance you might say! I had been
too preoccupied with work to bother
with women before. Even at University
I kept my head down in my books.
Alison seemed different from any girl
I'd ever met. She was bright, clever and
attractive, and she was into computers
too — like her brother so we had lots
in common, or so I thought.

'One day I received a telephone
call from a relative — an aunt down
in London had been burgled. She
sounded terribly distressed. I had to
go to her as she had no-one else to
turn to that I knew of, and she was
getting on in years. My partner said
he could look after things while I was

away — the project was about finished, it was mainly a matter of finding a buyer. We had hopes of selling it to an American outfit and since Alec was a far better salesman than me I went, leaving Alec as I thought to finalise the deal.

'My aunt was so shaken up by her experience that she had to go into a Nursing Home for a spell and I arranged for new security locks, etc. for the house. It ended up that I stayed away for over a week what with one thing and another.

'For the first few days that I was away I rang Alec daily and everything seemed fine — at least he answered the phone and we chatted normally. But then I started getting the answering machine whenever I called. I didn't think too much about it at the time because Alec always rang me back later and I knew that he didn't like being distracted when he was busy.

'When I finally returned home it was to find that my two compatriots had taken all the information regarding our project and fled to America.' His lips curled contemptuously. 'They certainly did look after things! They'd wiped my computer entirely clean and taken all the back-up copies of our project, leaving me absolutely nothing!'

'How awful,' Holly said, thoroughly shocked at such behaviour. She didn't quite understand what he meant entirely but she understood enough to realise the vindictiveness of it. 'What happened? Did you manage to track them down? Where did they go?'

'There wasn't much point in going after them. It wouldn't have done any good. It would have been my word against theirs and I couldn't prove anything. I never heard any more from either of them. The American firm didn't go ahead with the deal after all, but I have since seen a similar project being marketed under a different name.' He threw his hands out expressively. 'So now you know why I am security conscious these days, and why I'm not overjoyed at using an answering machine.'

'Yes, I can understand that,' Holly said vehemently. 'I hate to think of people like that getting away with it though. Wasn't there anything you could do?'

'I'm afraid not. It took me some time to realise what a fool I had been,' he declared. 'It wasn't only the loss in monetary terms, but the way I had been misguided enough in trusting people. I suppose in a way I could condone Alec for his part, he had after all worked on the program, but I thought Alison loved me, or at least was fond of me. I felt badly let down by her behaviour more than anything, because she was the only girl I'd had anything to do with romantically.

'I accepted that it was a mistake from which to learn a very valuable lesson. I'm sorry I snapped at you, Holly the other day, but that is why — the thought that you might have upset my office. However unintentional, you could have unwittingly lost some of my work. I have a comprehensive backup system now so it's hardly likely though.'

Holly looked down at her plate, realising now why he had been so angry and that she would have felt annoyed too if she had been in his place.

'Anyway,' he said with a rueful smile. 'Two years ago I came to live at the cottage with the thought of becoming a recluse. I had my work to keep me busy and that was sufficient. Cassie was a marvellous neighbour, she was there if you know what I mean — never intrusive and I knew she wasn't after my work!'

'And you want me to sign the official secrets act before you'll trust me into your holy of holies is that it,' Holly said, more sharply than she intended, feeling guilty because she had misunderstood his anger.

'No, Holly, don't get me wrong,' he said, covering her hand gently with his own rather large one. 'I know I can trust you in that way after Cassie's recommendation, but as a female you could very well lead me astray. You look remarkably like Alison in many ways, especially from a distance. She had short fair hair like yours, she was reed slim and about as tall as you, although she wasn't anyway near as pretty.

'You have a fresh, lively quality about you, an eagerness to please and be liked which isn't all that difficult to do. I suppose I have been rebelling at my own natural desire to have your company. I still haven't learned to trust a woman unless they are old enough to be my grandmother,' he grinned disarmingly.

Holly could well understand how he had felt about her meddling as he saw it. She was about to tell him so when a party of people passed their table, and one of them stopped abruptly.

'Duncan McCall! So what brings

you out into the big wide world? I've
been trying to contact you, hoping you
might honour us with your presence.
Daddy wants to meet you.' The woman
bestowed a wide smile on Duncan
who had got to his feet politely to
greet her. 'Don't tell me this is your
cleaning lady!' the woman chortled,
then glanced icily at Holly. 'I say, why
don't you join us.'

The rest of her party had by this
time carried on to a table at the far
side of the room. Holly stared down at
her plate, hoping that Duncan wouldn't
accept the invitation. She would have
recognised the voice anywhere.

'We are about to leave,' Duncan said
quietly. 'Another time perhaps?'

'Surely, darling. I'll keep you to that.
Don't forget to ring me soon.'

The woman swished over to her
friends and Duncan grimaced ruefully
at Holly, who for her part squirmed
inwardly at such an affected female
display.

'I forgot to tell you that a woman

rang while you were away on Tuesday but since she wouldn't leave her name I didn't mention it to you.'

'And did you by any chance intimate that you were my cleaning lady?' Duncan's mouth wavered with amusement.

'I guess I did. I didn't know what to say because I didn't know who she was.' The colour rose in Holly's cheeks. 'I'm sorry, I hope I haven't spoiled anything for you.'

'Not at all. You have probably done me a great big favour.' He was now grinning openly.

'Chloe Hunter-Johnson is one of the merry band of divorcees in the area who have tried for the past two years unsuccessfully to entangle me in their web.' Then he burst out laughing. 'A cleaning lady indeed!' His chuckles brought a smile to her lips and she joined in until they were both rolling with laughter.

'Come on, Holly, let's get out of here before they throw us out. I've never enjoyed a meal so much for a long time.'

He was still chuckling as they drove home. As he drew up outside his garage door he asked her if she would like some coffee.

'That would be a nice way to end the evening I think,' she said warmly.

'Oh, Holly, you are good for me.' He leaned over and kissed her lightly on the cheek. 'Would you mind opening the garage door and I'll put the car away.'

'What's that, bribery?' she said as she quickly stumbled out of the car, her face burned where he had kissed her, and she felt all funny inside. She wanted to know how it felt being held in his big powerful arms, he felt so comfortingly dependable. It had been no more than a peck on the cheek but it set her wondering what kissing him would be like. It would be quite an experience she thought, especially when he was in a light hearted mood like he was at present.

By the time he had put the car away she had her feelings back under control, and she hoped that her face didn't betray her thoughts. She wondered if it was the isolation that was making her feel vulnerable. In Prescot she'd had her own flat for four years, so was used to being on her own but she had known that her folks were not far away. She had also dated boys before, mainly workers from Bensons, but there had been nothing serious — nothing that set her heart a flutter as it was now.

She thought back to her last boy friend and compared him with Duncan. She realised that Duncan was all man while Jason had been a mere boy by comparison. Duncan would make an intimidating predatory male if he set his mind to it, not like Jason who had to steel himself to even kiss her goodnight! She had never been out with anyone quite like Duncan McCall. He was something of a puzzle, but he had definitely stirred up emotions in her which were unsettling to say the least.

Duncan went in first to disconnect the alarm and catch hold of Shep who was roaming freely about the house.

'Come along in, Holly. Why don't you choose some music while I make the coffee? As a mere man I think I can say that I can at least make a decent cup of coffee.'

'Is the other door connected into your alarm system?' Holly asked as she followed him into the sitting room.

'No. That's completely separate because Cassie wasn't happy about using it. I only put it on when her cottage was empty which wasn't that often. Latterly, Cassie didn't even go down to the village unless I took her in the car. She didn't worry about intruders the way I do. I've got a thing about it now I guess.'

He disappeared into the kitchen to make the coffee leaving her again regretting not visiting her aunt for such a long time, he knew more about her aunt than she did.

The room was tastefully furnished

with a leaf green carpet and gold velvet curtains at the window. A long settee of soft beige leather faced the fire with two easy chairs either side and a low coffee table conveniently placed in between. A bookcase along one wall was overflowing with books and magazines; plants were dotted about the room giving it a cosy lived in feel. Shep reappeared and flopped down on the hearthrug making it a homely atmosphere. The overall effect was very pleasing and restful.

Holly investigated Duncan's large selection of cassettes and found his taste similar to her own. They were mostly classical pieces, so she chose a selection of Mozart sonatas to play.

'Do you like the classics then?' asked Duncan carrying in a tray to put down on the coffee table.

'Yes, I do. I love all Mozart, Chopin and Beethoven, particularly Chopin — he's my favourite I think.'

'A woman after my own heart,' he quipped. 'Coffee's ready, come and find a seat. I would have thought your taste would be for the modern pop stuff.'

'I don't see why. Just because I'm young doesn't mean I have to conform to what everyone sees as the image of the youth of today.'

'No, of course not but somehow I never envisaged you with a classical taste.'

'I'll have you know my Dad used to take me to concerts when I was little — when he had the time that is.'

'You continue to surprise me,' he replied, his lips twitching with amusement. 'That can't have been so long ago — sorry I forgot, you said you were now a fully grown up twenty-two year old.'

She could tell he was teasing her so she refused to rise to the bait. She sat on the settee while he took an armchair, stretching out his long legs towards the fire in a casual, carefree fashion.

'I must say you do make a mean cup

of coffee,' she acknowledged, sipping it nervously, her feelings were all haywire in the intimacy of his snug room. Never had she felt such tension inside her than she did now, after one peck on the cheek! It was a totally new experience, leaving her confused and strangely excited.

At one point she realised that in other circumstances she would feel quite vulnerable being alone with a man in his house miles from anywhere. With Duncan it was different, it felt perfectly all right. He treated her as he would a sister — more's the pity. He obviously saw her as being too young to be romantically attractive and he was taking his promise to her aunt seriously.

'That is something I have plenty of practise at. When I get involved on a project I sometimes spend all night working, sustained by coffee and the odd sandwich. Time flies by when I get to my computer.'

'The nearest I got to a computer was

when they installed word processors in the office at Bensons,' Holly remarked. 'They were a big improvement on the old typewriters.'

Then they spent some time chatting about the merits of various composers before the conversation once again turned to computers and he explained a little about the project he was working on at the moment. Most of it was way above Holly's understanding but she enjoyed listening to him as he expounded on his work.

His voice had a lovely warm quality. He looked like a big cuddly bear when he relaxed, she thought but despite his size he didn't appear to be fat — merely broad and muscularly fit. When the music ended a little while later Holly got up to go, albeit a little reluctantly.

'I ought to be going, we cleaning ladies have to be up early,' she joked, and was rewarded with another chuckle.

'Thank you, Holly, for a most

enjoyable evening. I hope we can do it again sometime.'

'Yes. That would be nice. I've enjoyed it too.'

Picking up her coat she walked along to the connecting door hoping he would kiss her goodnight, but he didn't. He politely held the door open for her and wished her pleasant dreams.

That night she lay awake wondering what it must be like to be in love with someone like Duncan McCall. She remembered the light butterfly kiss he had planted on her cheek with exquisite rapture. She tingled with happy thoughts — he felt so wonderfully reliable. It was so strange how she had changed her mind about him in the course of one day.

What a pity he thought of her in a brotherly way, making fun of her youth and immaturity. But who knows what time may bring, she thought? After all he wasn't that old! Ten years difference in their ages wasn't too much surely.

5

The next morning Holly sang as she prepared breakfast for herself and fed Sooty. Her heart was deliriously light, everything in the garden was lovely. She should have trusted her aunt's judgement. Mr McCall was quite charming. OK, he had bad moods but didn't every one? After all, he had been badly let down so she could understand his aggression in a way now that she had heard his story. After what he'd been through she could understand his antagonism towards women, but maybe she could change his view of her.

Since it was another sunny day she set off on a sketching session, only this time taking the car round to the far side of the loch. The day went in haze of activity as she churned out her drawings avidly. Now that she was feeling pleased with life everything seemed to fall into place, and she discovered she was working so much better. She also found that instead of landscapes, it was the wildlife that attracted her.

She wished she knew where her ability lay. In which direction should she go if she was to make a living at it? Until now she had only doodled for her own enjoyment, but to make it a career one had to specialise in something that people would pay for. Her savings wouldn't last forever — she would have to do something to earn her living.

She rifled through her sketch pad and came across the sketch she had done of Duncan, then the ones of birds and thought that perhaps she should concentrate more on people and animals rather than full landscapes. Then she came up with the idea that if she could draw animals she could illustrate children's books, a bit like Beatrix Potter had done.

Maybe even write stories for children too! It would be something she could do when the weather was poor and she couldn't get outside. The new prospect excited her tremendously and she wished she could talk to Duncan about it to see what he thought, but she was loath to disturb him when he was working.

Back at the cottage she settled in front of the fire with a pot of tea, making a few notes and trying to come up with ideas for children's stories. She racked her brains until she had to admit defeat. Maybe tomorrow something will come to me she thought, as she climbed into bed with Sooty snuggled up beside her. She was glad to have his company and told him of her plans.

'What do you think old boy? What would aunt Cassie have me do?

The weather turned inclement. A cold, clammy mist descended keeping Holly indoors. She mooched about the cottage churning over in her mind possibilities for children's books. Then she remembered the numerous exercise books she had filled while she had been staying with her aunt as a child, and wondered if they were still around. They would be a good source of information.

She hadn't gone into her aunt's bedroom much since she had taken over the cottage but perhaps, she decided, it was about time to go and clear it out. It was no use putting it off — it was something which she would have to do sometime, even though she knew it would be distressing. After all if she didn't do it nobody else would.

Sadly she pulled open the wardrobe and began stacking her aunt's clothes into bags to give away, feeling despondent about the lonely life her aunt had led. Next, she tackled the dressing table drawers, carefully keeping the few items of personal jewellery separate, thinking her mother might like some of it. When she came to the last of the chest of drawers she found it stuffed full of papers, books and photographs.

Taking the drawer downstairs she settled in the sitting room to go through it, hoping that she would find her old exercise books there. The first thing she unearthed was a bundle of letters tied up with fancy red ribbon. She frowned in puzzlement. She had never thought of her aunt being in love with a man — she was the typical elderly spinster — she always had been!

Putting them to one side she next took out a photograph album and a box full of old snapshots, these she also put to one side to go through later at her leisure. Finally she came to a cardboard box and there were all her books, drawings and childish scribbles faithfully preserved. Her aunt had kept everything she had ever done by the look of it. Holly flicked through them with a smile when she saw the childish handwriting and immature pictures, they immediately transported her back in time to her youth. Yes, this was what she wanted! The very thing!

That afternoon she sat at the kitchen table busily scribbling away revamping her childish stories with ideas for sketches to go alongside. She was quite enthusiastic now, she felt she had found her way forward to a promising career. Ideas spilled out on to the paper one after the other.

The next day she went into Kirkston to have a look around the book shops, especially children's books to judge the market and what competition she would be up against. She purchased one or two, then went to have a cup of coffee before doing the rest of her shopping. She was deep in thought mulling over what she had seen. She felt sure she could do something equally as good.'

'Hello, Holly. Mind if I join you? I saw you coming in here.'

'Please do, Mr Andrews,' she said quietly, removing the packages from the seat next to her, feeling there was no alternative since he had taken her unawares.

'Malcolm, please,' he reminded her.

'How is the world treating you, or should I say your next door neighbour?' He grinned at her in a friendly fashion, his big round face beaming broadly.

'Oh, we're getting along fine now thanks, Malcolm. In fact we don't see much of each other but we are on amicable terms — a sort of truce if you like.'

'I'm pleased to hear it. Only . . . ' He looked at her thoughtfully. 'Holly, I don't know whether I should tell you this.' He paused again resting his hand against his cheek. 'I heard something the other day about Mr McCall. I don't like passing on idle gossip, but since it concerns your next door neighbour I thought maybe you ought to be aware of it.' He frowned as if unsure about his wording.

'Go on then tell me what you've learned,' she pressed him, now more than a little curious. 'What guilty secret have you discovered?'

'Now, I really . . . I shouldn't . . . ' he stopped as if having second thoughts.

'Oh, go on,' she urged feeling irritated by his reticence now he had her attention. She wanted to know what he had heard if it involved Duncan.

'Look, I'm not completely sure of the validity — it is only hearsay you understand, but it's possible that Mr McCall is married.' He sat back stirring his coffee absent-mindedly watching Holly's reaction to the news.

'Well, that is no sin is it?' she said as nonchalantly as she could manage although her spirits plummeted with the news. An icy tingle ran down her spine when she thought about her more recent hopes regarding Duncan. 'I haven't seen any sight of a wife though, not while I've been here.'

She tried to make light of it, but it had come as a body blow. She daren't even drink her coffee for fear of spilling it. She felt all of a dither.

'No, I gather she walked out on him after a very short time and no one has seen or heard of her since. But look, Holly, please don't mention any of this to anyone else will you? I shouldn't have told you but I don't want you getting over friendly with the man. I don't want you to get hurt. Something about the man tells me that he's bad news.'

'That's all right I won't tell a soul. There's not much to tell anyway is there if you're not sure if it's true?' she assured him getting quickly to her feet, eager to be alone with this new information. 'I will have to be getting along as I have work to do. 'Bye Malcolm.'

'Good-bye, Holly. Don't forget to look me up next time you're in town. If there is ever anything I can do don't hesitate to ring me. You have my number haven't you?'

Holly blundered out of the cafe and back to her car feeling completely numb. Why had she assumed he was single? After all he was definitely good looking — too handsome to be still available surely. She sat for a long time staring out of the windscreen feeling cold and miserable inside.

It was all spoiled again just when she thought everything was turning out fine. She thought back to everything Duncan had told her — no there had been no mention of his being married to Alison or any one else for that matter. Maybe, if he had married Alison and she had walked out on him like he'd explained, he was hardly likely to want to broadcast it was he?

Finally she switched on the engine and motored home in a daze not bothering to do any shopping, she wanted to be alone with her unhappy thoughts. She was dismayed to find that she cared — she really cared, and that if the truth were known she must be a little in love with Duncan McCall. She took herself bitterly to task telling herself that she hardly knew the man and that he could be an unbearable monster at times, how could she be in love with him? But it didn't ease the sadness she felt. She was as forlorn and miserable as the weather.

'Holly, would you mind taking calls for me?' Duncan asked the next morning. 'I shouldn't be too late back I hope.'

'Sure,' she said disconsolately. 'No problem.'

'Are you all right, Holly?' he asked, tipping her chin up with his index finger and peering into her face. 'Not sickening for something I hope.'

She couldn't meet his eyes. 'I'm fine thanks. Got a lot on my mind that's all.' She hoped she sounded more convincing than she felt.

He left with a brooding look on his face and Holly slumped down on the kitchen chair unhappily. What on earth was she going to do? With her equilibrium so disturbed she couldn't make any progress with her stories, and yet she couldn't bring herself to ask him outright about his marital status. It was none of her business anyway, and he would no doubt tell her so in no uncertain terms. By tea-time she hadn't made any useful progress but papers littered the kitchen table when Duncan returned.

'Had a busy day?' he asked, idly picking up some of the sketches. 'These are very good — quite professional.'

Holly sighed and gave him the telephone messages.

'You're not looking too happy, Holly. Have I offended you somehow? If so it is purely unintentional I do assure you.'

'No, it's nothing,' she lied.

'Look, how about joining me for a bite to eat?' he said in an effort to cheer her up. 'You haven't anything prepared have you?'

'No, I don't know. I'm not very good company at the moment,' she said wearily, sweeping all the papers together in a dispirited fashion.

'Come on, I won't take no for an answer. Grab your coat and let's go. I'll bet you haven't eaten all day and I need to eat anyway even if you don't. Come and keep me company.'

Holly felt torn both ways. She wanted

his friendship and she would like his advice but she knew that she was becoming too fond of him. That would be a mistake in view of what Malcolm had told her so she ought to keep her distance.

She found herself being hustled out of the door without being given chance to even put a comb through her hair or change out of her scruffy jeans.

'I'm not dressed for going out anywhere,' she protested half-heartedly.

'Not to worry, we won't go anywhere fancy.'

By the time they took their seats in a small unpretentious cafe in Kirkston Holly was feeling decidedly hungry and her stomach rumbled ominously. As he had surmised, she had been too pre-occupied with her thoughts all day to bother about food and being with him lifted her spirits. Duncan was obviously a regular at the cafe and the proprietor made them both most welcome.

'Now, what have I done to upset you this time?' Duncan asked while they waited for their meal. 'I thought I had been on my best behaviour — a model neighbour in fact, so what's the trouble?' He smiled engagingly at her troubled face. 'What can I do to help?'

'It's not you that's the problem,' she said crossing her fingers under the table. 'I have decided to try my hand at illustrating children's story books but now that I have seen the competition I'm beginning to wonder if I will be any good at it.'

'Is it something you really want to do? Cassie told me you wanted to paint.'

'I have always liked painting but until now I have only dabbled in my spare time. I don't know yet what I will be any good at. The other day when I was clearing out Cassie's things I came across my old exercise books full of childish literary works that I did years ago. She'd kept them all and I thought they would make the basis for a book, which I could illustrate,' she tailed off, full of self doubt and misery.

'Well, you'll never know until you try so if that is all that is bothering you, then why the long face? You have to knuckle down and give it your best shot. It sounds like a good idea to me.'

'I suppose it must be the wet weather that has got me down a bit,' she reflected. 'I've never had so much free time on my own. It seems so strange not having to go out to work — not meeting people, or being at their beck and call. It takes some getting used to.'

'Yes, it most certainly does,' he replied stretching out to take hold of her arm consolingly.

'You know, if you ever get lonely you can always come and help me. I'll find you a job.'

'You said you liked your privacy,' she reminded him as her heart lurched alarmingly — the touch of his hand sent her into a dither. Sparks seemed to be exploding within her. It wasn't right to feel like that about a married man, but she couldn't control her feelings. He had said to think of him as a brother but that wasn't how she saw him at all. For the first time in her life she felt herself to be in love and it had to be with a married man — it wasn't fair.

'Yes, well, that was before I met you. You seem somehow different — anyway I promised Cassie,' he added rather quietly.

It was pleasant talking to him — he was being so friendly and amiable that she resolved to do as he suggested and try to get a book put together. She wished she dare ask him if he was married but she couldn't find the right way to frame the question. Oh, why had Malcolm Andrews told her of his suspicions? She had been so much happier not knowing. The only thing to do was to get out and meet other people and try to think of Duncan in terms of big brother as he'd suggested in the first place. She knew it was going to be difficult but she would have to make the effort.

Holly's resolve to join in the village activities came the following week when she found they were holding a jumble sale in the village hall. The people who ran the post office store mentioned that they could do with some help man the stalls, so she immediately volunteered. The school needed some more equipment which she thought a worthy cause.

She donated a few items herself, and quite enjoyed being a stall holder, it meant she met some new faces and was asked out to tea by some friends of her aunt. They were mostly much older than her unfortunately but at least it was a start. She was particularly pleased to note that the paintings which she had donated sold.

At the jumble sale she met the local school teacher, Peter Metcalfe, and when he learned that she was a secretary he asked if she would like some part time work, helping him with a thesis he was doing.

'I've just completed it but now it has to be typed up. I was going to see if I could get someone in Kirkston to do it. Would you mind? I'd pay you what you thought reasonable.'

'I'd be delighted to do it if you in turn will show me round your school. I wanted to come here as a child,' she said 'but of course I couldn't. I envied the children in the village for having such a lovely little school right on the doorstep.'

'You're welcome to come and look around anytime. We don't get many visitors, and the children would love it.'

After that Holly spent some time each day at the school, either talking to the children, showing them how to paint or typing Peter's thesis. She thoroughly enjoyed it. It got her out of the house, meeting fresh faces as well as doing something useful. It didn't stop her thinking about Duncan but it helped by keeping her occupied.

She was going to do the typing at home but found it easier to work at the school, so that when she had difficulty in deciphering Peter's handwriting she could ask him straight away. Peter had written about Kirkston, concerning the changes the arrival of the railway had made to it and how its people had adapted to the changing industrial environment. It was a fascinating manuscript and Holly often remained after school closed to work on it. Peter stayed most nights to mark exercise books instead of taking them home to do.

He was a quiet, inoffensive man, in his early forties she guessed and still a bachelor. He appeared to be a good teacher, if somewhat strict with the children but they seemed to respect him for it. He brooked no nonsense from them but he was fair. When Holly handed him the completed manuscript all neatly typed he diffidently asked her if she would like to go out for a meal as a way of showing his gratitude.

'Thank you, Peter,' she replied unhesitatingly. 'That would be nice.'

'I'm afraid I don't have a car,' he said.

'Oh, that's OK. I'll meet you in Kirkston if you like. I don't mind driving there one evening.'

'If you are sure you don't mind? I usually cycle everywhere.' He looked so shy and reticent.

'How do you cope in the winter months?' she asked, trying to put him at his ease.

'On bad days I catch the bus, or sometimes I get a lift from friends if they are coming this way. It's really not too bad and the exercise does me good.'

Holly arranged to meet him the following Saturday evening in Kirkston High Street. It turned out to be a cold night so she decided to wear one of her office suits with a pale lemon blouse and a warm cape over the top for when they were walking to the restaurant.

'Off out again?' Duncan startled her

as she was locking up. 'You're never in these days.' He sounded bad tempered and critical she thought. He'd obviously just arrived home, his car was still on the driveway with the engine idling. She hadn't seen or spoken to him for days. Ever since she learned that he was possibly married she had kept out of his way as much as possible, too confused by her own emotional state to want to get involved.

'I've been invited out for a meal that's all,' she said coolly, wondering if he kept note of her comings and goings. Maybe he was annoyed because she wasn't there to take his messages she thought. He made no further reply and Holly stalked off to her car annoyed at his belligerent attitude. It was no business of his what she did or who she went out with. She was a free spirit and could look out for herself.

Peter was extremely well mannered and escorted her with great politeness to one of Kirkston's smartest hotels where he had booked a table. Holly hadn't expected anything so grand and felt pleased she had worn her dressy suit. Peter looked slightly embarrassed and fingered his tie nervously. She smiled thinking he looked very dashing in his Sunday best, even though he obviously found it uncomfortable. More used to a sports jacket than a suit she surmised.

'This is lovely,' she said, once they were seated at the secluded corner table. 'But you shouldn't have gone to so much trouble. It looks extremely expensive.'

His hand shook as he handed her a menu. 'I wanted to make a good impression. I am grateful for all your work, Holly, and for taking such an interest in . . . the school.'

Throughout the meal they chatted mostly about his work and thesis. Once she got him talking he seemed gratified to have an audience willing to listen to his scholastic life story. He told her about his love of books and seemed genuinely interested when she told him about her own aspirations. He said he was probably going back to college again, he had enjoyed teaching but he preferred the academic routine. He was waiting to hear any day if he had been accepted.

Holly wished she could have paid her share of the bill but he wouldn't hear of it.

'This was my treat and you deserve it, Holly.'

When they left the hotel they found it had started to rain. It was a real down-pour so she offered him a lift.

'If it won't take you out of your way, thank you I'd appreciate it, although it isn't far to my place, I could easily walk.'

'Come on, hop in, you'll get soaked in no time in this. You give me the directions. I'm not too familiar with this area you know.'

The wipers had difficulty keeping pace with the deluge and soon the windscreen misted up making it even more difficult seeing where they were going. Holly drove cautiously following

Peter's directions.

He guided her to a shabby Victorian property converted into numerous flats where he occupied one on the top floor. The rain eased off fortunately as they drew up outside.

'Would you like to come in for a minute?' Peter said. 'Coffee perhaps? I have some pictures you might like to see of Kirkston in the early nineteen hundreds.'

Normally she would prefer to have gone straight home, but after her contretemps with Duncan she decided she would give him something to think about and be out late for a change.

'Thanks. I'd love to,' she said switching off the engine. Peter seemed so delighted to have her company and Duncan wasn't her gaoler for heaven's sake. She wasn't sure why she was deliberately trying to annoy Duncan but felt somehow irrational where he was concerned.

They made a dash for the front steps and Peter ushered her up several flights of dingy stairs to the top floor. His flat was rather drab and only sparsely furnished. It could certainly do with a good sweep and clear up was her first impression. He directed her into the small sitting room, clearing away books and papers from the settee in order that she could sit down.

'Here is the book I was telling you about.' He rifled through a stack on the floor. 'The pictures are quite revealing about life in Kirkston in the early part of the century. I'll make the coffee. Won't be long.'

Holly took the proffered book and glanced briefly through it, then looked about the room feeling rather sorry for Peter. After twenty years of work he hadn't much to show for it. It could certainly do with a woman's touch, even a few pot plants would brighten it up. It was so cheerless compared to Duncan's cosy arrangement — she automatically made the comparison.

The room was only small and even though Peter had switched on an electric fire it still felt cold and depressing. The rain which had become quite heavy again, beat against the window adding to the gloomy atmosphere. She shivered, wishing that she had kept her cloak on instead of leaving it in the car, but she hadn't realised how cold it had become.

Perhaps she ought to be going, it was getting rather late and maybe it wasn't such a good idea staying out late in such conditions. For some reason she was uneasy. Peter came back with the coffee, motioning her to take a seat again.

'What do you think of the book?' he asked putting the tray containing two odd beakers and a plate with a few digestive biscuits down on the stool next to her. Sitting beside her he showed her some of his favourite pictures, his arm surreptitiously sliding along the back of the sofa, and coming to rest on her shoulders. She flinched feeling mildly panicky although not quite sure why. She shuffled further along the settee trying to put some distance between them, but his hand shot out and gripped her. She found herself being crushed against his chest hardly able to breath. He was much stronger than he looked.

'You know, Holly, you are extremely beautiful. I've never met anyone quite like you before. No one else has ever listened to me like you have.' He seemed both excited and nervous at the same time. 'I'm truly honoured to have your company.'

'Please, Peter,' she cried struggling to free herself. 'I'd better be going. It's late. I ought to be getting home.'

'Oh, don't go yet. I thought we were getting to know each other. And you haven't had your coffee.' His voice went an octave higher, his eyes held a gleam of bravado. The precious book slithered to the floor but he made no attempt to retrieve it.

Holly now became really scared. 'But I must. I only came for coffee,' she stammered. 'I have to go. It's late.'

He smiled, a rather sly smile. 'That's what you say, but your eyes tell a different story. I saw the look you've been giving me all evening, and why else did you stay late after school? I could tell that you . . . ' His hands started wandering down over her blouse.

She shrieked as he attempted to undo the top button. 'Please, Peter. Stop it. What's got into you? I have to go. This is all a mistake.'

She tried to get to her feet but he held on tight, trying to pull her against the cushions. His hand got tangled up in the strap of her shoulder bag, pinning her arm back for a moment. By now she was thoroughly frightened as she had never been before. In the ensuing tussle a button tore off her blouse and the tray containing the beakers tipped to the floor with a clatter.

Holly lashed out viciously in blind panic. Finally managing to free herself she ran to the door, jerked it open and fled down the stairs as if the devil himself was after her. Fortunately for her she still held on to her bag containing the car keys. Instinct must have made her cling to it as they'd struggled. She was sobbing with dismay by the time she clambered into her car and hurriedly locked all the doors. Only then feeling safe enough to give way to tears. It was several minutes before the shivering stopped and she felt calm enough to start the engine.

She didn't remember much about the journey home, Peter's behaviour had upset her to such an extent that she drove like an automaton. She had thought him a shy individual and only wanted to be friendly with him. She couldn't understand what had got into him. She didn't remember driving through the village or along the lane. When she arrived back at the cottage she was still dithering with fright.

After locking the car she scurried down the path towards the cottage and when Duncan loomed up out of the gloomy garden she jumped with a startled cry, for some unknown reason thinking it was Peter.

'Sorry, I didn't mean to frighten you. Not very gallant I must say, leaving a lady to return home on her own at this time of night,' Duncan mocked. 'I don't think much to your choice of company!' He turned to go into his own front door, whistling for Shep who bounded down the lane.

Holly stood by the porch desperately looking for her house keys but in her upset state she couldn't find them. She tried her pockets and her handbag to no avail. She was about to go and see if she had left them in the car.

'You all right, Holly?' Duncan turned back when he heard her sob. 'Lost your keys?'

It was all too much, she burst out crying.

'Hey, whatever is the matter? You look really upset. I'm sorry, I didn't mean to cause offence. Come on, Holly. Come along in and tell me what's been going on.' Calmly he took her by the arm and led her unprotesting into his sitting room. Even with only a table lamp lighting up the room she could feel his eyes noting her dishevelled appearance, and she pulled her jacket together to cover up her torn blouse, suddenly conscious of the state she was in.

'Holly, what on earth happened? Who did this to you?' His controlled anger very apparent, he made no attempt to approach her but stood gripping the back of the settee, his eyes blazing.

Eventually she managed to pull herself together sufficiently to explain. 'I've been out to dinner with Peter Metcalfe — the school teacher. He wanted to repay me for doing some typing I did for him. We went to the Astoria where we had a lovely meal.' She bit her lip. 'I gave him a lift home because it was raining and . . . and he invited me in for coffee. He said . . . He seemed . . . I only wanted to

131

be friendly. He said I'd been making eyes at him, and that I encouraged him to think . . . '

'Holly, for goodness sake, have you no sense! You honestly don't realise what you're doing do you? You obviously have no idea how your *friendliness* can be misinterpreted as a definite *come on*. The poor fellow must have thought it was Christmas. But still, that is no excuse for the state you're in. Has he touched you? Are you all right?'

'No, I'm all right now thanks,' and she truly meant it. Now she was with Duncan she felt safe. 'It was a bit of a skirmish that's all, and I panicked. It must have been something about his flat. It was sort of seedy and I felt uncomfortable.'

'Would you like a drink to calm your nerves? Or a coffee maybe?'

She managed a wan smile. 'A coffee would be nice. It got knocked over at Peter's. I hope I'm not taking you from your work?'

'No, that's all right. I was taking a turn outside when I heard your car coming down the lane. I shan't be a moment. Make yourself at home.'

Holly tidied herself up, fastening the buttons on her suit jacket to make herself more respectable. Then she tipped her handbag out to try to find her house keys. They weren't there. Where could she have lost them? She went over in her mind where she had been and hoped that she hadn't lost them in Peter's flat. The thought of having to see or meet him again appalled her.

'Steady on,' Duncan said as she tried to hold the cup of coffee and it spilt, her hands were shaking so much. 'You're a bundle of nerves.' He set the coffee down on the table.

'I've lost my keys. I can't find them. I'm sorry. I don't know what's the matter with me.' She ran her hand through her hair. 'I had them earlier tonight before I went to the restaurant obviously, because I locked up. At least, I think I locked up.' She frowned trying to remember locking the door.

'Drink your coffee and then we'll investigate,' Duncan said calmly. 'Have you left the connecting door undone by any chance?'

'I can't remember that either. I'm sorry.'

'OK. You sup your coffee while I have a look round.'

She heard Duncan try the connecting door without success and then he went outside with a torch. A short time later he came in with her keys dangling from his finger.

'Here you are, young lady. You left them in the door.'

6

The next weekend Holly had a surprise visitor — her cousin Roger. He arrived very early on the Saturday morning quite out of the blue.

'Your parents asked me to look you up since I was going to be in the area. I would have rung to let you know I was coming if you'd been on the telephone. How is life in the sticks, young Holly? I had the devil's own job finding the place.'

She grinned with amusement, delighted to see him. Roger was four years older than her but they had always got on well together. He treated her like a younger sister, hugging her enthusiastically and whirling her round like a child.

'Let me have a look at you. Definitely not eating enough, which reminds me I haven't eaten for hours. I hope you can remedy that forthwith, and in return I will unload the goodies your parents have entrusted me with.'

Holly laughed out loud. 'I'll go and put the kettle on.' He was what she needed — a real tonic.

Soon they were reminiscing at the kitchen table while Roger had his second breakfast of the day with Holly helping him out with some of the toast.

'How are things, young Holly?' he asked. 'Seriously, I mean. It is rather off the beaten track here isn't it? You're miles from civilisation.'

'Everything is fine, honestly. You do like to exaggerate. I would like your advice though.'

'Fire away, my love. Anything I can do to be of assistance, just ask. That's what I'm here for.'

'Well, I suppose Dad told you that I wanted to become an artist, and since I came here to live I have made a start — you might think I am being silly but . . . I came up with the idea of publishing a children's book.'

'That sounds like a smashing idea. What's the problem?'

'I don't know how to go about it. I mean I have made a start on the story and the illustrations, but how do I go about finding a publisher, all that . . . ?' Holly tailed off with a frown.

'Let's see what you've done so far and I'll give you the benefit of all my vast experience,' Roger grinned good naturedly. 'It will cost you a bed for the night though.'

'What luck I made up the spare bed only the other day — I must have known,' she replied.

Holly cleared the table and gave Roger the work she had done so far then let him browse through it while she washed up.

'These look great,' he said expressing genuine admiration. 'When I get back to the civilised world I'll see what books I can find which might help you if you like. You know — how to find a publisher and what sort of material are they looking for, etc. I presume you have looked in the local library.'

'There wasn't much of any help there, I'm afraid.'

'Come on, grab your coat, I could do with a walk,' he said leaping to his feet. 'I've come to see what you find so appealing about this place. From what I've seen so far it certainly isn't my scene but maybe with you as my guide — who knows?'

The weekend went far too quickly. All too soon it was Sunday afternoon and time for Roger to leave. Holly felt very grateful for the boost in confidence he had instilled in her. It had been marvellous out walking and talking, dropping into pubs for refreshments and chatting until the early hours by the fireside.

'Not a bad little place,' admitted Roger as he stood at the garden gate prior to leaving. 'That is, if you like this sort of thing, but I would soon be up the wall wanting the bright lights, I'm afraid. I can see why it appeals to you though, Holly. I'll report back that you are well and truly settled, and there's nothing to worry about shall I?'

'Please,' she said earnestly. 'I don't want my folks worrying about me.'

After Roger left she decided that she ought to do something about the spare room in case she had other visitors. She had automatically used the small back bedroom which had been hers as a child, but now she owned it all so it was time to make changes. The furniture was old and cumbersome and when she compared her cottage with Duncan's she realised that it did need modernising. She didn't want to delve too deeply into her savings but with a bit of careful planning she felt she could at least afford to brighten the bedrooms up quite a lot.

She resolved to get more organised, so the first thing the next morning she went into Kirkston to arrange for someone to make her an offer for the heavy old fashioned furniture. Then she purchased some paint, quickly ducking into a doorway when she saw Malcolm Andrews walking towards her. Fortunately he hadn't seen her and she managed to scuttle back to her car unobserved.

By the end of the week she had transformed her aunt's bedroom. With the old furniture out of the way Holly painted the walls a delicate pink which toned in nicely with the rose carpet, and she bought some attractive floral curtains and a counterpane to match. The double bed she kept, but now there was much more floor space and she had visions of a small kidney shaped dressing table in front of the window, with a flouncy curtain skirt and the alcoves boxed in like Duncan's for use as wardrobes.

* * *

Shep appeared in her bedroom one morning while she was still asleep. The first Holly knew was when Sooty started spitting angrily making Shep bark in retaliation.

'Shep? What are you doing here?' she said rubbing her eyes sleepily.

She grabbed hold of Sooty to calm him down then struggled into her dressing gown to investigate how he'd got in. She knew something must be wrong for Shep to arrive like that.

Duncan stood at the bottom of the stairs already dressed complete with anorak.

'I'm sorry to disturb you so early, Holly, but I've had a call to say my father's been taken ill. I want to be under way soon. I wondered if you would hold the fort for me and keep an eye on Shep?'

'Yes, of course. That's no problem. I'm sorry to hear about your father. I hope he'll soon be better.'

'Thanks.' Duncan frowned. 'Not expecting guests this weekend are you?'

'No, I don't think so. At least I hope not as I have the spare room upset at the moment. I'm doing a spot of decorating.'

'Take care,' he said as he turned to go. 'Don't go falling off any step ladders or anything will you while I'm away?'

Somehow he seemed cold and distant with her she thought. Was he merely concerned about his father or had she offended him somehow? She tried to put it out of her mind but it wouldn't go away. It niggled continuously because she didn't think she had done anything to cause offence. The fact that Duncan had keys to get into her cottage also surprised her. She hadn't realised that he had them — he'd never said. Even when she thought she'd lost her own he hadn't mentioned them.

She decided to decorate her own bedroom too now that she had got started and she wanted to get it finished as quickly as possible so that she could get back to her book. The money she got from the sale of the furniture was far more than she had expected, so she felt she could afford to employ a joiner to finish the bedrooms off. She had already made enquiries at the village store and been given the name of someone to contact. Having arranged for him to do the work starting early Monday morning she wanted to be all finished painting by then. She was putting the final touches to the paintwork in her bedroom on the Saturday morning when the phone rang.

When she answered it there was nobody there. Cursing whoever it was for having disturbed her she went back to her painting, grumbling about such ill mannered people. A short while later the phone rang again. This time however a woman asked to speak to Duncan and she seemed a bit put out because he wasn't available.

Holly asked if she would like to leave a message but she declined and she wouldn't even leave her name. When she put the phone down Holly sat brooding about who it could have been. Could it possibly have been Duncan's wife? It certainly hadn't been Chloe Hunter — she'd have recognised her voice again without a shadow of doubt. Somehow the phone call irritated and upset her.

Half an hour later the phone rang again. This time in her haste to run down to the kitchen where she had left the mobile phone she tripped up over Sooty who had a habit of sleeping on the stairs.

She was puffing a bit when she answered.

'Holly, are you all right?'

'Yes, Duncan, at least I think so. I've fallen over the cat. I'm sorry it took so long to answer, but I was upstairs. I'd left the phone on the kitchen table.'

'You're sure you are all right?' he persisted.

'Yes — no bones broken. How is your father?' By now Holly had got her breath back and was rubbing her side, she knew she would have a lovely bruise where she had caught herself on the hall table.

'He's much better, thank you. I rang to say that it looks as if I will have to stay until the early part of next week. I hope to be back Monday night, but it may well be Tuesday.'

'That's OK. Shep is fine and there was only one message yesterday for you — a salesman trying to sell you some electronic gear by the sound of it. He said he would catch you another time.' She paused momentarily. 'A little while ago the phone rang twice in quick succession. The first time there was no-one there, but the last time it was a woman. She asked for you but when I told her you weren't here she wouldn't leave a message and rang off.'

'Hmm,' he said. 'No clue at all?'

'She sounded young,' Holly replied brusquely. 'She said you'd know who it was if that is any help, because you'd met her only last Tuesday. All very mysterious I must say.'

'Oh, that's all right then. Nothing to worry about. I'll ring her back.'

After reassuring him that she wasn't

thinking of going anywhere, that she was perfectly all right on her own and promising to keep the doors securely locked at all times, he rang off.

Holly spent the afternoon clearing up ready for the joiner and finally went for a bath. The bruise was a multi-coloured affair and it was quite tender but it hadn't broken the skin luckily. It's a good job it's not bikini weather she mused absent-mindedly as she relaxed in the hot suds contemplating what Duncan thought of her. The anxiety in his voice had been very touching and she reflected on their up and down sort of relationship. And who was the mysterious woman who'd rung that morning? Was it his wife? That thought made her feel miserable so she tried to forget it.

Duncan McCall is quite a complex character she declared to no one in particular. She wished she knew what really happened but she couldn't ask Duncan, and she couldn't think of any other way of finding out. There were certainly no photographs about his cottage that she had seen. The woman, whoever she was had a lot to answer for, fancy leaving a man like Duncan. She knew she wouldn't have if it had been her.

It seemed awfully quiet at the cottages by herself, and she wondered how her aunt had coped for so long. As far as she knew aunt Cassie had lived there all her life — nearly eighty years! Holly shuddered at the thought. She loved the cottage, but at times she did feel lonely and couldn't envisage staying there on her own forever.

On Sunday, Holly didn't feel in a working mood. Since it was pouring with rain she settled beside the fire with Shep and Sooty, who seemed to have settled their differences and were content to share the hearthrug. She took out her aunt's letters and photographs, unwrapping the ribbon rather warily. She disliked the idea of reading such personal correspondence but felt that she couldn't discard them without first seeing if there was anything of relevance which ought to be kept.

The date on the envelopes showed they were written some fifty years ago. The letters were artistically written in a beautiful flowing script, addressed to 'My Dearest Cassie'. They were tender, affectionate love letters from someone called Gordon and they were obviously very much in love with each other. At first Holly thought how wonderful it was that her aunt had found such a charming man, but then her pleasure turned to anger at the way he had finished the affair.

The story Holly managed to piece together made her feel deep sorrow for her aunt, and fury with the man called Gordon for the shabby way he had treated her. It looked as if aunt Cassie had fallen deeply in love with Gordon and even borne him a child — a son. Gordon had bought the cottage for Cassie and her son to live in, but unfortunately the baby died when he was only three months old.

The letters tailed off after u̶ tone became cold and apath last letter was a curt note to ȷ his wife had learned of their al̶ and he would have to terminate t̶ relationship.

Poor Cassie, Holly sobbed, tears springing to her eyes. To think that anyone could treat her so despicably! Aunt Cassie, who had been such a gentle soul — so kindly disposed to everyone. How anyone could hurt her like that? She wondered who Gordon had been. Had he been a local person? Maybe nobility even with too much to lose by leaving his wife for the woman he loved. He obviously had loved Cassie in the beginning at least, the letters were so romantically phrased.

Tearing the letters up Holly burned them one by one, realising how little she had known her aunt. What a shame her son hadn't lived to be a comfort to her she thought sadly. She put the photographs away to have a look at another time. She was far too upset

nore of the past for

you, Sooty old boy,' up the cat to nurse

Thursday Duncan ...tchen where Holly ...y working on her book. He thrust the portable phone at her.

'Somebody called Roger for you.' Disgust emanated from him like a thunder cloud. 'I trust you will ask before giving my number to anyone in future.' With that, he fumed out, slamming the connecting door violently behind him.

'Roger? How did you get this number,' Holly asked.

'Sorry, love. I gather I've boobed. I heard what he said. I remembered you mentioning his name when I was with you the other weekend so I looked him up in the telephone book. I only rang to ask if it would be all right for me to come up again tomorrow?'

'Oh,' she said. 'Yes, of course you

can come.' She felt upset by Duncan's mood, and even Roger's cheeriness couldn't lift the gloom that descended upon her like a wet blanket.

'Could I bring a friend too?' Roger asked. 'I think you'll like Steve.'

'Sure,' Holly said rather absent-mindedly. 'The more the merrier. After all it is a double bed.'

She heard Roger chuckle making her wonder if he was trying his hand at matchmaking again. She'd had problems with Roger in the past trying to fix her up with a suitable boy friend.

'See you late tomorrow night then, all being well. Sorry to get you in hot water with your neighbour but I'll put it right at the weekend, never fear. Maybe we could all go out for a meal somewhere to make amends?'

'Perhaps,' she agreed half heartedly. The mood Duncan was in he wouldn't be very good company even if he accepted Roger's apology. It was some little while later when she finally plucked up courage to go and return the telephone to Duncan. Since his return from visiting his father he had been coldly formal whenever they happened to meet. She thought perhaps it had been the phone call from the woman that had upset him although it didn't seem to bother him at the time.

'I'm sorry about that,' she said nervously nibbling her bottom lip. Duncan was irritably striding about his lounge looking thoroughly disgruntled. 'I must have mentioned your name when Roger was here — that was how he managed to find you in the 'phone book.'

'Huh,' he growled.

'Roger is my cousin,' she went on quietly. 'He only rang to see if it was all right for him to bring a friend for the weekend. I'm sorry if he disturbed you, and he also apologised. He would like to make amends and suggested we all go out for a meal together.'

'Your cousin?' Duncan said gruffly. 'Well, there's no harm done. I was in the middle of something, that's all. The 'phone distracted me.' He managed a weak smile. 'Sorry I was such a grouch.'

'That's OK. He shouldn't have rung like that. I'm sorry he bothered you.'

All day Friday Holly spent cleaning and baking, she knew that Roger had a healthy appetite and expected that his friend Steve would also. By early evening she was feeling a little jaded but the thought of Roger's company boosted her morale. She had a quick bath and since he was bringing a guest she decided to put on a dress instead of her usual jeans and sweater, thinking it would make a better impression. She wondered who Steve was. Did he work at the same firm as Roger and was he planning on pairing her off with him?

It was nearly ten o'clock when she saw the lights of a car approaching down the lane. She had almost given them up as not coming after all. Putting on the outside light she waited in the porch, and was somewhat startled to see a young woman emerging from the passenger seat of Roger's car.

'Hi, Holly,' Roger called cheerfully. 'Sorry we're so late. We got lost. Blame my incompetent navigator. Can't trust her to find her way out of a paper bag.'

The woman laughed gleefully as he tucked his arm round her waist and escorted her down the path.

'Holly, I'd like you to meet Steve. She's my boss's daughter so we have to keep on the right side of her,' he grinned.

Holly was staring bewilderedly from one to the other.

'I . . . I only have one spare bed,' she stammered. Quickly backing into the hall she led the way into the sitting room, feeling her colour rising at the awkward position Roger had placed her in. She had no idea what the relationship was between them but she didn't approve of people sleeping together before they were married and certainly not under her roof!

'Roger, would you show . . . Steve,' she faltered over the name. 'Show Steve the bedroom while I put the kettle on.' She frowned grimly at him, hoping that he would get the message that she wanted a word with him in private.

'Right ho,' he said. 'This way, milady.'

Holly heard them laughing as they went upstairs and she went into the kitchen feeling furious with her cousin. Roger appeared a short time later and she turned to face him, her arms crossed trying to contain her anger.

'What is the meaning of this?' she demanded. 'You knew I took Steve to be a man. Why didn't you tell me?'

'I know, honey. I'm sorry. I didn't do it intentionally, but when you assumed I meant a man friend I saw the funny side. It's short for Stephanie you know. If it suits you better I'll go get a bed for the night in the village.'

'You know you'll not be able to get a room at this time of night. You can jolly well sleep on the settee.'

'Whatever you say. I don't suppose it's much good asking your next door neighbour is it?'

'No, I don't,' she snapped. 'He hasn't got a spare bed anyway.'

'And how do you know that may I ask?' he said cheekily. 'Maybe I had better not.' He didn't quite make it out of the kitchen before the tea cosy missile hit him.

★ ★ ★

Saturday didn't start out too well. Holly woke up with a thumping headache. She cursed when she remembered her guests. She went to get a couple of aspirins from the medicine chest in the bathroom and then climbed back into bed. They can jolly well get their own breakfasts, she muttered snuggling down again.

Stephanie was a stunning beauty — no doubt about it. Petite but with a perfect hourglass figure, flawless complexion, exquisitely dressed and

156

definitely a man chaser — it oozed from every pore of her body. Holly thumped the pillow angrily when she thought about the expensively tailored trouser suit Steve had been wearing so coquettishly. Immediately she wondered what Duncan would make of her. Stephanie was the sort of woman who could wrap men round their little finger, even Duncan wouldn't be immune, she suspected.

Eventually she drifted off to sleep again. It was ten o'clock when next she woke. Dragging on her dressing gown she went to see what her guests were doing, thinking it was uncommonly quiet. Roger wasn't one for silence. He would no doubt have the radio on or the tape recorder if he was up and about.

To her surprise she found the sitting room door open and the blankets neatly folded on the settee but there was no sign of Roger or Stephanie. In the kitchen she found a note saying that they had taken themselves off for a walk since it was such a beautiful day.

Holly put the kettle on and made herself some toast, grateful to have the time to compose herself.

'You OK, Holly?' Duncan seemed to appear before her as if by magic. She had just been thinking about him.

'Sure,' she said grumpily. 'A bit thick headed that's all.'

'I met your cousin this morning.' Duncan looked quite chirpy so she wondered what had been said. Maybe it was the sight of Stephanie that had got him in a good mood, she thought miserably.

'I agreed to a foursome this evening, if you feel up to it.'

Holly couldn't have cared less about going out that evening. 'Fine,' she muttered.

'You don't look particularly happy,' he remarked. 'Is there a problem?'

How could she tell him what the problem was? How could she explain her feelings when she didn't understand them herself? She felt annoyed that it distressed her to think of him being already married, and she was jealous of Stephanie with her sophisticated womanly ways. Why did her emotions get tangled up at the sight of him? Why couldn't she calmly accept him as a good neighbour and nothing more?

'No problem. I feel an idiot that's all. When Roger said he was bringing a friend called Steve I expected a man, and Steve turns out to be a woman.' Very much a woman she nearly added. 'As you know I only have one spare room!'

'I see,' he said solemnly. 'Do I take it you disapprove of the modern promiscuous attitude to sleeping together outside marriage?'

'What if I do?' she snapped irritably. 'I know it's an old fashioned attitude but so what?'

'I totally agree with you,' he replied quietly. 'Look, while they're out why don't you take it easy. I have to go up to the farm for some eggs, do you want me to get you some? On second thoughts, why not come with me?'

Duncan had a way of making his suggestions sound like an order, not that she need any second bidding anyway, she welcomed the chance to be with him. She knew it was weak of her, but she wanted to grasp every opportunity that arose. Married or not she enjoyed being with him.

'Come on, Holly. See you outside in five minutes. It'll do you good, a walk in the fresh air.'

She practically threw on some jeans and a warm sweater, picked up her anorak and went to meet him. She didn't even take time to powder her nose, not wanting to keep him waiting.

The walk to the farm helped clear away the remnants of her headache and since Duncan appeared to have got over his grumpiness it was really enjoyable. He seemed very much at home in the country, his observation of the wild life was most remarkable. He stopped her more than once en route to quietly watch an animal which she would have passed without noticing. First a rabbit in the hedge bottom, then a squirrel scampering up a tree, and most impressive of all an owl, so well camouflaged as to be almost invisible.

His eyes seemed to spot anything that moved, and even those that didn't, and he was genuinely interesting to listen to. He told her about his fascination for nature ever since he was a small boy and had a way of explaining that made her wish she had known him then.

She would love to have joined him on his rambles, bird watching and making friends with the animals. He told her how he had been given Shep who had been injured in a road accident and he had nursed him back to health. Shep certainly looked fit now as he scampered on ahead of them every so often leaping into the hedge bottom.

Unfortunately, the more Holly was with Duncan the more unhappy she became about her feelings for him. She had never accepted the casual way some of her friends had about seeing married men, having scorned them for their lax moral ways and yet here she was doing exactly that. She tried to treat him as a friend or brother, but her emotions ran high whenever she was with him.

On their return, she settled in the kitchen to look at the bumf which Roger had brought — the promised books and a couple of writers magazines which he thought might be helpful. They certainly gave her food for thought.

It was late afternoon when Stephanie and Roger returned.

'Hope you didn't mind us going off like that,' said Stephanie flopping down on a chair and kicking off her shoes. 'It was such a lovely day. Roger's walked me off my feet, I'm whacked. We've walked for miles.'

'You must think me a poor hostess,' Holly said. 'I didn't realise . . .'

'I know,' Stephanie grimaced and stretched up to give Roger a light clip round the ear. 'Your cousin here has a warped sense of humour, I'm afraid. He's the only one who ever shortens my name to Steve. It's become like a pet name.'

'I think Stephanie sounds much nicer,' Holly replied.

'Ganging up on me now, are you? It's as well your neighbour is joining us tonight then, I can't manage both of you at the same time.' He grinned unashamedly.

Stephanie's ears pricked up with interest. 'What's he like, your neighbour?' Her perfectly groomed eyebrows rose delicately and if she had been a mouse Holly could well have imagined she would have preened her whiskers.

'Oh, he's quite a dish,' Roger said giving her a hug. 'What a pity you are stuck with me!'

'Is there anything I should know?' Stephanie asked Holly, her eyes dancing excitedly as she escaped from Roger's clutches.

'No,' Holly said vehemently. 'Duncan McCall is my neighbour, nothing more.'

'Sure?' Roger said mockingly. 'OK. OK. I get the message.'

Stephanie glided out of the room saying she must have a soak in the bath and prepare herself for the evening's entertainment, leaving Holly wishing that she could plead a headache and retire to bed. She had no wish to witness Stephanie making eyes at Duncan, or to see her cousin upset even though he thoroughly deserved it. She had the impression that Roger liked Stephanie more than he was letting on, and she knew that if she pulled out then ten to one Stephanie would somehow arrange for Roger to stay behind too, so she could have Duncan all to herself.

'Fancy a cup of tea,' she asked Roger, noting his subdued expression once Stephanie had left the room.

'Please,' he said pulling out a chair to sit down. 'Have I put my foot in it again, Holly? I really didn't mean to.'

'Why do you ask that?' Holly said deliberately averting her face as she filled the kettle, wondering whether she ought to mention that Duncan was possibly married, then thought better of it. Malcolm had asked her not to tell anyone. She doubted if it would make any difference to Stephanie anyway.

'Steve's a man-eater, I know. She always has to be the centre of attention. She will no doubt go after McCall tonight and I must say he looks to be quite a catch. Just Steve's sort. Although I shouldn't want to get on the wrong side of him, he looks as if he can handle himself all right.'

'So? Don't you care?' Holly said turning the tables on him. Roger's words felt like a knife being turned in her chest, sharp and poignant. She was plainly jealous of Stephanie's worldly wise attitude.

'No, Steve and I are using each other. I like the high life as you already know, and Steve happens to find me acceptable as an escort for the time being. It's not love or anything like that, my dear cousin. We're friends. Going about with the boss's daughter boosts my esteem no end, and she's great fun most of the time, even if a little spoilt. Mind you, when she finally grows up she might be worth waiting for.'

* * *

Holly chose to wear a delicate lavender coloured dress and high heeled shoes, knowing full well that she would tower over Stephanie, making her feel like an amazon next to a wood nymph. There was nothing she could do about her height so she may as well make the best of it, and in any case, no doubt Stephanie would get all the attention.

She grimaced at herself in the mirror as she brushed the tangles out of her hair, the walk that morning had made it spring into tighter curls than usual and she hadn't had time to shampoo it, Stephanie having spent so long in the bathroom that Holly barely had time for a quick wash.

Duncan offered to drive them to the restaurant since he knew the area, and Stephanie jumped into the front passenger seat before Holly had even locked the cottage door. Holly climbed into the back next to Roger without saying a word but she noticed Duncan's set face — he hadn't approved! One point to me, she thought gleefully.

Throughout the evening Stephanie monopolised the conversation as Holly had expected. She surprised Holly with her knowledge of computers, and since her father's business was engineering she managed to keep Duncan fully entertained. Stephanie wasn't such a dizzy blonde apparently. She liked to give that impression in order to have men's attention it seemed but underneath she was a force to be reckoned with.

To give him credit, Duncan did try to include them all in the conversation as much as possible but Holly spent most of the evening sparring with her cousin. She found herself reminding Roger of episodes from their past, trying to keep him from dwelling too much on Stephanie's bad manners as she openly flaunted herself at Duncan. Holly had a hard time hiding her own feelings of animosity at Duncan's obvious attraction to her guest, he was being perfectly charming. So much for not being interested in the opposite sex, she thought mutinously!

On leaving the restaurant Duncan deliberately it seemed, assisted Holly into the front seat while Stephanie struggled with the hood of her coat. A light drizzle had begun and she didn't wish to ruin her hair-do. Duncan grinned at Holly in the light from the central display as he helped her with the seat belt, a look of mutual understanding making the evening more bearable.

Holly thought about the night he had taken her out to the King's Arms — that had been so wonderful.

What a pity it had gone wrong since. She cursed Malcolm Andrews for his untimely gossip, even though she knew that she was being unfair on him. She shouldn't get involved with Duncan if he was married, that was one thing she didn't approve of, even if his wife had deserted him. She would have to stop her feelings getting out of control by finding other outside interests. Go to night classes, beetle drives or flower arranging, anything to get out meeting others, although since the Peter Metcalfe episode she had been a little reluctant.

'Fancy coffee?' Duncan asked as they drew up outside the cottages again. Roger and Stephanie were already getting out of the car.

'Lovely,' Stephanie called over her shoulder, as she made a dash for the porch.

'Shall I open the garage door for you?' Holly asked, grinning mischievously.

'Please, that would be a help.'

She hesitated for a moment, wondering if he would remember, then leaned over and kissed him lightly on the cheek. 'Thanks.' She leapt out of the car before he had time to ask what for. 'I'll see if my fire is all right. Won't be long.'

Leaving Roger and Stephanie to go with Duncan, Holly went into her own cottage. She needed a few minutes to get her emotions under control. Whatever had possessed her to kiss him, in front of the others too! Although they probably hadn't noticed, they were sheltering from the drizzle. She knew that she had been annoyed because Duncan had spent so much time with Stephanie and she was feeling a little piqued. Duncan had looked surprised though, she thought with a grin.

Holly went through the hall door as Stephanie happened to be exiting Duncan's kitchen, where she had no doubt been *helping* him make the coffee.

'My, that is useful, isn't it? I didn't

know that door opened. I thought it was all sealed up.' She smiled maliciously. 'How very convenient for intriguing assignations!'

'It was put in for my aunt Cassie's benefit,' Holly remarked sharply.

'Of course, *I* believe you!' Stephanie said snidely. 'Thousands wouldn't though. Well, I mean — '

'Holly's, quite correct,' Duncan retorted, coming from the kitchen to join in the conversation. 'I had it put in so that I could keep an eye on her aunt more conveniently.'

'Why of course, that made sense *then*,' Stephanie acknowledged. 'Still, it's different now isn't it? I mean . . . What do you think the neighbours would say, if you had any that is?' she sniggered.

'Holly usually has the bolt on at her side,' Duncan growled, his face thunderous at the insinuation. 'Now, come and have the coffee before it goes cold.'

The atmosphere in the sitting room

was distinctly frosty with Duncan looking furious, Holly red with embarrassment and only Roger it seemed his usual self. He had been browsing through Duncan's music cassettes so hadn't heard the conversation.

'Thought you might be going to the exhibition in Edinburgh, Duncan?' he remarked casually. 'It's in your line I should imagine. Our firm is going to be represented.'

'I've got plenty of work on at the moment to keep me going well into next year, so I don't think I'll bother,' Duncan replied, in rather an off-hand way.

'Why on earth do you want to stick in this place in the back of beyond?' asked Stephanie. 'Why not expand if you have so much work on?'

'Not everyone wants to live in the city, Steve,' remarked Roger, sensitive of Holly's feelings. 'Some people like the simple life and the charm of the countryside.'

'I can't think why. Except of

course they have to make their own amusements.' Stephanie flashed Duncan a knowing look. 'That might be where the *charm* lies!'

'The sort of work I do can be done anywhere and since I find peace and solitude to my liking this seems to be an ideal place,' Duncan said slowly as if choosing his words with care. 'As to expanding, I've tried that and found it unsatisfactory so I'll paddle my own canoe in future. More coffee anyone?'

Holly sensed the undercurrent of restraint in his voice and quickly remarked that it was perhaps time they were leaving. They said their farewells and retired through the hall door with Stephanie gleefully telling Roger how convenient it was when they didn't have to go out into the rain to come in again.

Holly got ready for bed feeling dispirited by the way the evening had gone. Stephanie had tarnished the atmosphere with her innuendoes. She lay awake thinking for quite some time before turning off the light. She had never felt vulnerable with Duncan, even when he had complete access to her home — she knew him to be too honourable to take advantage in any way, because of the special circumstances of his friendship with her aunt.

There was something about him which made her feel completely confident that she could rely on him, although she couldn't put her finger on what gave her that assurance. Maybe, she thought, it was remembering how he'd sent Shep up to waken her the morning his father was taken poorly. He could equally well have come himself since he had keys to let himself in but he hadn't come to her room.

She was dropping off to sleep when she heard a floorboard creak and stealthy footsteps on the stairs. With a sigh, she wondered who was prowling about, but had no wish to investigate and make a scene so she buried her head in her pillow and tried to shut out her thoughts. If Roger and Stephanie wanted to sleep together it was none of her business, even if she did feel it inappropriate under her roof, there wasn't really anything she could do about it.

What did get her out of bed with a bound was the alarm being set off. She grabbed her old velour dressing gown from the back of the door and hurried to see what was going on. It was the first time it had gone off since she'd arrived and inadvertently set it off herself.

At the bottom of the stairs she came upon Stephanie in a diaphanous negligee holding a hand to her head as if in pain. Roger, with a blanket round his shoulders was emerging from the sitting room, and apparently, on the other side of the connecting doorway was Duncan.

As he switched off the alarm everyone started talking at once.

'I was coming down to have a word with Roger about something and I must have opened the wrong door by mistake.' Stephanie, her face red with anger was trying to explain how she had accidentally set off the alarm.

'Couldn't it wait until the morning?' Roger asked sleepily.

'How come you had to take the bolt off to open the door if it was a mistake?' Duncan asked coldly and seeing Holly, raised his eyebrows questioningly.

'I . . . I don't know. I don't remember. Yes, I do. It wasn't on,' snapped Stephanie triumphantly. 'That's it — it wasn't on.'

Holly shrugged her shoulders. 'I can't remember if I put it on or not now.' The whole scene made her feel sick — Stephanie wearing practically nothing and resorting to such a weak excuse, she must know nobody believed her but she didn't appear to care.

'Nobody told me about the alarm anyway,' said Stephanie smugly. 'It frightened the life out of me when it went off. You should have warned me. I might have had a heart attack.'

'What was it you wanted to see me about that was so important?' Roger stared fixedly at the floor looking embarrassed.

'I can't remember now. It's gone completely from my mind. I can't think. It's got me all confused. I'm going to bed, I'm freezing.' Stephanie scampered away.

Roger shrugged his shoulders and returned to the sitting room, muttering incoherently something about *dizzy women*.

'Glad to see *you* managed to find your dressing gown, Holly,' remarked Duncan dryly. 'Maybe we had all better get back to bed. Sleep well.'

She noticed that he had only discarded his tie and obviously hadn't turned in yet. Had he been expecting a nocturnal visitor she wondered as she slowly trudged back upstairs. It took her ages to get to sleep after that. She couldn't stop wondering what would have happened if the alarm hadn't been on. Would Duncan have welcomed

Stephanie into his bed? Didn't the fact that she had come with Roger matter? Round and round her thoughts went until finally she slept.

Holly was the first to surface the next morning and made herself some tea. She was about to make some toast when Roger wandered in, sleepy-eyed and yawning.

'Tea — super.' He slumped down on a chair and accepted the proffered cup and saucer.

'Sleep well?' Holly asked wryly.

'Not particularly,' he grunted. 'That settee isn't all that comfortable. It's not long enough for a start.'

'Serves you right,' she snapped, getting out the butter and marmalade and extra crockery.

'Sorry about last night, Holly,' he said sheepishly. 'Steve went too far.'

'Possibly,' was all Holly could manage. She was still feeling livid about Stephanie's remarks and general behaviour all weekend. She wanted to feel sorry for her cousin but she couldn't because she felt he had brought it on himself.

'Good morning everyone,' Stephanie burst into the kitchen, warmly clad in a long quilted dressing gown. 'I thought I was the first up. Isn't it a beautiful morning?'

Holly was staggered by her apparent brazen attitude.

'Would you like a cooked breakfast?' she asked politely, remembering that Stephanie was her guest, however unwelcome.

'Oh, no thanks. I'll only have tea and toast. Duncan's going to show me his computer set-up this morning,' she smiled smugly. 'I don't want to keep him waiting.'

'Actually, old girl, we're all going,' Roger said instantly wiping the smile off her face.

'I didn't hear him invite you along,' Stephanie replied sulkily.

It was the first Holly had heard about it too, but she wasn't inclined to refute her cousin, thinking maybe he was trying to be diplomatic in view of the previous night's fiasco. Stephanie must be thick skinned if she couldn't see how upset Roger was with her behaviour. Although, how she could confront Duncan she would never know — she knew if it had been her she would have run a mile rather than meet him after last night's scene.

'I didn't think computers were anything in your line?' Stephanie said looking from one to the other, to be met by blank expressions.

'I'm interested in the technical stuff he does on them,' Roger said by way of an explanation.

'I'll give it a miss, I think,' Holly said. 'It's not my cup of tea, but invite Duncan to join us for lunch if you like.'

Roger scowled at her but she didn't care. It was all his fault for bringing Stephanie in the first place, but it had shown Duncan in his true colours. As far as she was concerned she was fed up with the lot of them, and she didn't wish to spend more time than she had to with any of them.

As she peeled and chopped the vegetables Holly's thoughts went back to her childhood. She thought about how she'd helped her aunt prepare the traditional Sunday lunch with such meticulous care. Life had been so simple and uncomplicated then. Maybe I am naive, she thought, maybe Duncan's right, I am a child still emotionally, too scrupulously moral for my own good for which she had her aunt to thank. She sighed, she had a lot to thank her aunt for and no mistake. Cassie would have made a wonderful mother with her thoughtful ways, gently guiding and teaching in such simple fashion. What a terrible shame her son hadn't survived.

Lunch was rather a fraught meal for Holly with Stephanie hanging on to Duncan's every word and making no attempt to pacify Roger who was looking more than a little put out.

Duncan didn't look too displeased by Steve's obvious interest which incensed Holly still further. Towards the end of the meal the talk became more general and Stephanie happened to mention that she knew someone who lived nearby whom she wished to visit.

'That's what I was coming to tell you last night, Roger. I suddenly remembered, and wanted to see if you would take me to see them. We could always drop in on our way home — that's if we are not too late setting off.'

'Where do they live?' Roger growled, obviously miffed, his patience about run out.

'This side of Kirkston I believe — by the loch side I was told. It's called 'Hunters Moon' of all things.'

'Don't tell me you know the Hunters?' Duncan's eyebrows shot up in surprise.

'Why yes,' she simpered. 'Do you know them?'

'Huh. Sort of,' replied Duncan with a sniff of disapproval.

'Why, what fun,' declared Stephanie. 'We could've invited Chloe to join us last night if I'd known.'

Holly noticed Duncan's face tighten and she smiled vindictively at the thought that Stephanie had really put her foot in it this time.

'You'd have gone on your own then,' Duncan murmured.

After that Stephanie became deliberately annoying and silly, remarking that Chloe was someone she had met on holiday, and the two of them had struck up an immediate rapport. She couldn't think how anyone could possibly dislike her. She flounced out of the kitchen leaving the three of them in bemused silence.

'Well, what was all that about?' asked Roger. 'I gather you don't particularly like Ms Hunter?'

Duncan merely smiled and shrugged his shoulders dismissively leaving Holly to answer her cousin's veiled question.

'I think you should make up your own mind when you meet her,' she said diplomatically. 'All I can say is that she is hardly likely to become a friend of mine. Now, shoo both of you, so that I can get on with the washing up.'

Roger and Stephanie left shortly afterwards, Stephanie looking distinctly cool. She managed to thank Holly for a pleasant weekend with a total lack of sincerity. Roger hugged her, apologising for his ill mannered passenger, and said he was sorry he had spoilt her weekend. 'I'll come on my own next time. That is if I haven't blotted my copy book irredeemably.'

'You're always welcome, Roger, you know I think of you like a brother so I guess I have to accept your quirky behaviour from time to time. Thanks for the books by the way, I think they'll be a great help.'

Duncan waved to them from his front porch. 'I'd best get back to work,' he said, as Holly walked back down the path.

'Maybe you should,' she snapped.

He frowned. 'Anything wrong?'

'What could possibly be wrong?' she sniped sarcastically.

'I thought I had been helping you entertain your guests.'

'Guest you mean!'

Holly couldn't bear it any more, she walked on into the house and slammed the door shut behind her. She ought to have remained in Prescot, she thought dispiritedly. What did she think she was doing staying here in Struan? Maybe she ought to admit she was no artist and return home.

7

Holly went for a long walk by the loch. It was a cool damp day and yet she felt she needed to get out. Following the episode with Peter Metcalfe she was more cautious about getting involved in the village activities, and her thoughts constantly strayed too often to Duncan for her own peace of mind. What did she know about him? He might have umpteen girl friends for all she knew, despite what he said about preferring solitude. He often went out for an hour or so in the evening, ostensibly to take Shep for a walk, but maybe he had a lady friend to call on. Where indeed was his wife, and who was the woman who rang while he was away?

Holly had been walking for quite some time. It didn't seem to be helping. She still felt miserable and depressed. The path gradually meandered towards the road where she found a wooden bench seat. She stopped to admire the view and rest a while, and sighed at the sheer beauty which even the cloudy day couldn't hide.

She wished that she was more at peace with herself. Her thoughts were a jumble — a chaotic shambles. She had got over her irritation at the way Duncan had treated Stephanie. Once she thought calmly on her own she realised that he had been as polite as she might have expected. It had been days since she'd seen him, and she missed him.

A bright red sports car careered noisily along the road, and screeched to a halt a short distance from her. A young man leapt out. 'I say, are you local?' he enquired.

'I guess I am,' replied Holly, smiling at him in her usual amiable way, expecting he wanted directions. He looked a very personable young man, dressed in stylish, casual clothes, and he had a friendly, open face.

'I thought I knew all the pretty girls around here,' he said flirting with her, and without a by your leave took a seat next to her. 'For a moment I thought I was back in Ireland and that you were a pixie or even a leprechaun.'

'Hardly a pixie!' Holly smiled at the absurdity. 'Not with my height.'

'The name's Alistair,' he said with a broad smile. 'And who may I ask, are you, fair maiden?'

'Holly — Holly Davison,' she said, grinning openly now at his engaging manner.

'I say, I am delighted to meet you. Can I give you a lift? It's about to pour down by the look of those black clouds up there. I shouldn't be surprised at a storm brewing.'

Holly hadn't realised how dark it had become, and glanced up at the darkening sky. 'Thanks, I would appreciate a lift to the village if it isn't taking you out of your way.' He seemed perfectly charming, and since it appeared he was a local she didn't think she could come to any harm. 'I live at the cottage down the lane, but if you could drop me off at the cross-roads I can easily walk the rest.'

'Wouldn't dream of it, my dear. I'll take you to your door, that way I have your company for that much longer.'

He was a real charmer thought Holly with some amusement.

'And what do you do, Holly Davison, when you're not day-dreaming by the roadside?'

'I'm a secretary, but since I came to live here I am dabbling at becoming an artist.'

'Fascinating. And what do you paint, may I ask?'

'At the moment I'm working on an illustrated children's book.'

'Golly. You are an enterprising pixie.'

Outside her cottage, she thanked him for the lift, remarking that it was fortunate he had come along when he did as it was starting to rain, and it did indeed look like it was set in for the day.

'Would you do me the honour of having dinner with me sometime?' he asked. 'I don't know many people round here. You're the first person I've met who isn't old enough to be my grandma.'

'I'd love to,' she replied, without a second thought. He seemed so charming and well mannered.

'How about tomorrow night? I'll pick you up at seven. OK?'

Holly agreed and went into her front door feeling on top of the world. Alistair had told her he was staying with his parents not so far away, at the end of the loch, and from the look of his clothes he was reasonably well off, so she felt he would be a pleasant distraction from Duncan. For a few moments she did wonder about the advisability of going out with a stranger again, but he had seemed so open and amicable, and hadn't expected her to go to meet him like Peter had. Although, she didn't know his last name, she suddenly realised.

The next evening Holly got ready for her dinner date with special care. She chose to wear a slim fitting sheath dress of delicate apple green, and a shortie imitation fur coat. She wondered where Alistair would be taking her, and hoped her outfit would be suitable. She felt certain Alistair would choose a reasonably high class establishment and she wanted to be dressed accordingly.

'I say, you are definitely an asset to the community,' Alistair declared when he arrived at seven on the dot. 'Where did you say you came from, my pretty maid?'

'Prescot.'

'Well their loss is Struan's gain, and that's for sure.'

He helped Holly into the passenger seat of his low slung sports car with exaggerated courtesy, and they sped off along the lane.

'I thought we'd go to the Castle. How does that suit you?' he asked as they raced, at what Holly thought was break-neck speed through the village.

'I must admit to never having heard of it,' Holly said, cautiously holding on to the seat in an effort to stay upright. She would have preferred a little less speed, especially through the built up areas, although he appeared to be a capable driver.

The Castle proved to be a discreet, though chic hotel on the outskirts of Kirkston. Holly's fears were allayed by the pleasant ambience as they were shown to a cosy booth in the softly lit dining room. The background music was subtle, not intrusive, and the other diners talked in subdued tones.

After they had given their order Alistair grinned mockingly at her. 'Now my little pixie, how about telling me your life story? I want to know all about you. I'm surprised you haven't been snapped up by now. I don't know what the young men of Prescot have been thinking about to let you escape like that. Have you left a trail of broken hearts down there?'

What a charmer, she thought, not

taken in by his glib tongue but enjoyed his teasing ways. As they ate she told him a little about her life in Prescot before inheriting the cottage. 'I don't remember seeing you when I came in my school days,' she remarked. She felt sure she would have remembered him if she had met him before. 'Have your family lived here long?'

'Not really. My parents bought the house — oh, about four years ago I think, but I've only visited on infrequent occasions, so I don't know many of the locals. This isn't my idea of a place to live — it's far too quiet and dreary.'

'Which house is it? There aren't many at the end of the loch.'

'It's called 'Hunters Moon'. My parents renamed it. I gather it used to be called 'Cairn Lodge'.'

'So you're Alistair Hunter?' Holly's eyebrows rose questioningly.

'Yes. That's right. What gossip have you heard that makes you look so apprehensive?' he asked quizzically. 'I do assure you that I am a completely honest and upright citizen, if somewhat lazy, so my father tells me. Granted I don't pretend to work exceptionally hard, but I make a reasonable living without straining myself.'

Holly chuckled. 'It's only, that I've met your sister Chloe — she's a friend of a friend. I didn't realise you were her brother.'

'That sounds intriguing, we'll have to go into that further sometime. Big sister didn't let on about knowing anyone in the area.'

The evening was a huge success as far as Holly was concerned. Alistair behaved impeccably and saw her home in the proper manner. She hesitated about asking him in for coffee, but decided not to, merely thanked him politely as they pulled up outside the cottages.

'Thank you, Alistair for a lovely evening.'

'I've enjoyed it too. By the way, since you know Chloe, would you care to come to a small cocktail do we're having, a week on Saturday?'

'Oh, I don't know,' Holly demurred, not too enamoured of meeting Chloe again.

'Oh, go on. Otherwise I'll be left to talk to all the old biddies my mother has invited. You'd be doing me a big, big favour if you came. Please say you will, Holly? I shall feel mortally unhappy amongst that gathering without your company. Please?'

'All right,' she capitulated, seeing his hound dog look. 'Although, I cannot promise to stay long.'

'Smashing. I'll come for you at eight o'clock sharp then.' He leant over and pulled her into his arms for a good-night kiss. 'Sleep well, my little pixie. Things are definitely looking up in Struan. You might even entice me to come and see my folks more often, now that you are in the neighbourhood. That will please them no end.'

Holly climbed out of the car and watched as he hurtled off down the lane, her face flushed with a strange kind of excitement. She had enjoyed the evening and even found his kiss quite pleasant, but it didn't make her tingle the way Duncan's had. She always found herself comparing her men friends with Duncan, and they came up wanting for some reason or another. She wished she didn't feel that undeniable attraction to him, but there didn't seem to be anything she could do about it.

'I guess he at least saw you home!' Duncan's voice broke into her reverie. 'That wouldn't be Alistair Hunter by any chance would it?'

'Yes, it was if you must know. He took me to dinner at the Castle. He was perfectly charming and I thoroughly enjoyed it,' Holly said rather sharply.

'That's all right then. You don't need a shoulder to cry on tonight, I take it?'

Instantly Holly felt remorse for her abruptness, it appeared he had been doing his big brother act, looking out for her in case of need.

'Sorry. I didn't mean to snap. Actually, he's asked me to a cocktail party at his house, and I was wondering what to wear.'

'My, we are coming up in the world, aren't we. I hope you know what you're doing, young Holly. The Hunters haven't exactly been accepted around here, despite splashing their money about.'

'I take people as I find them, and Alistair seems very nice.'

'A friendly warning, to watch your step, that's all.'

* * *

A couple of days later, Duncan asked her if she would like to go out with him.

'I feel like taking the day off and wondered if you would care to join me. I need to clear a few cobwebs away.'

'Love to,' she answered promptly,

despite the nagging voice telling her that it wasn't sensible. 'Where did you fancy going?'

'Let's meander and see where we get to shall we?'

With Shep flopped down on the back seat they set off in brilliant sunshine. Holly was feeling happy merely being with Duncan, she didn't care where they went. He seemed to be in a quiet, thoughtful mood, so she quietly watched the scenery and waited until he felt like talking. Soon they were travelling along unknown roads as they headed inland and then he turned off into a forest clearing.

'How about we stretch our legs and give Shep a run?' he suggested.

She agreed. It was ideal weather, quite warm for the time of year. It was pleasant walking along the track through the pine forest, throwing sticks for Shep to chase after, and for a while neither spoke. The sun filtered intermittently through the trees, and except for the trickle of water in the ditch, all was peaceful. Holly thought how wonderful it would all be if only he was unattached and available. He was so agreeable and friendly on such occasions. Out of doors and away from the office situation he was a different person altogether.

'Holly, I have something to divulge which is a little awkward,' Duncan said after a while. 'I might have unwittingly put you in some danger.'

She glanced quickly up at him to see if he was joking. It seemed such a strange thing to say in the circumstances. No, his face appeared set in a grim anxious frown. She wondered if he was going to admit that he was married, but that didn't make any sense either because that wouldn't put her in any danger.

'How?' she asked. 'I mean, what possible danger can I be in here?' she said waving her free arm to incorporate the whole area. 'Apart from my own stupidity that is. I realise how silly I was going to Peter's flat like that. I won't make that mistake again in a hurry.'

'No, I didn't mean that, Holly. I have a confession to make. I am an engineer as I told you, but also, I am at the moment aiding the Police in the course of their duties, I believe the expression is.'

Holly looked suitably startled. 'That sounds ominous. What on earth have you been up to, Duncan McCall? And what interests the Police in such a small, peaceful community as Struan?'

'I've not been up to anything unlawful,' he said with a wry grin. 'This in a roundabout way concerns a cousin of mine — a very bright young man by all accounts, although I rarely met him. He went to University where it was expected that he would do extremely well. Then he . . . he got mixed up with an unsavoury crowd — a girl was also somehow involved. We never found out if she was responsible in any way. Anyway during his second year at University, my cousin killed himself with a drug overdose.'

Holly looked shocked. 'Accidentally?'

'No, we don't think so.'

'Oh, what a terrible shame.'

'It was a complete mystery to everyone, because Gordon seemed to have everything going for him, and as far as we know had no worries of any sort. He was bright, talented and not short of money like most students. One theory was that he fell in love with the girl but she turned him down, and he took the drugs to find solace. It doesn't sound sensible to me. I can't think any woman is worth it.'

Holly listened quietly, not wishing to interrupt his flow, but she knew he was thinking of Alison. It looked as if the death of his cousin had affected Duncan deeply and he needed to talk to someone about it.

'Grandfather never got over it,' he continued. 'He sort of gave up on life, because Gordon was all he had in the world — all he had to live for it seemed.'

'You shared the same grandfather I take it?'

'Yes, Gordon's father and my mother were brother and sister, but my mother fell out of favour when she married someone her parents didn't approve of. However, when Gordon died grandfather extracted a promise from me, that if I could ever do anything to bring about some sort of restitution, I would do so. Drug users and drug pushers are an evil I cannot abide, so I agreed readily enough. It pacified my grandfather, and I didn't think there was any chance of my being in a position to actually do anything.'

'How does this concern me?' Holly asked at length, curious as to how it affected her since she hadn't known his cousin as far as she knew.

Duncan paused so long that she wondered if he was going to continue — if in fact he even remembered that she was still there. He seemed lost in a private world of his own. Eventually however, he did.

'The Customs and Excise people believe that there is an operation in our area. I got involved purely by chance. Sometimes, as you may know, I find it helps to go for a walk late at night. It aids the thinking process when one has a knotty problem to solve. I often walk along beside the loch, and until a few weeks ago I saw nothing unusual. There's seldom anybody about.

'The night in question I was walking along the back road, and saw some men acting in what I can only say was a suspicious manner. The next day I informed the local Police and thought that would be the end of it. However, they became quite interested and told me to report anything else I happened to see on my nightly outings. Being local I had more opportunity to be out and about and not draw attention to myself.

'After that I took more notice of anything at all questionable. Then, if you remember, you took a call on my behalf, when I was away visiting my father. That was my contact, wanting some more information about the men I'd seen previously. Apparently they have definite suspicions about certain parties but no proof, and wanted my assistance. They mentioned that it is possible that I am under scrutiny, and if that is the case then you might be also.

'I know this sounds all melodramatic and I don't want to scare you, Holly, but if you remember I did try to deter you from coming in the first place. However, being seen in public with me might have put you at risk. It's something I hadn't reckoned with. I don't want you involved. There's not a lot I can do about it now, but I should have realised at the outset and kept my distance.

'I don't suppose there is any use appealing to you to leave Struan for the time being, is there? Won't you even consider going back home for a month or two — say until after Christmas?'

'None whatsoever,' she declared, so pleased to hear that the woman hadn't been his wife that she felt over the moon with happiness. 'Perhaps you could explain a little more about the people you suspect, and maybe I could help. After all I have a good excuse for being out and about sketching and so on. I could keep my eyes peeled for anything suspicious.'

'That's what I was afraid of,' he sighed. 'I knew if I even mentioned it you would be all agog to get involved. I shouldn't have said anything, only it has been a damned nuisance ever since you bolted that door. Sometimes I used to leave by Cassie's back door so that I could use the hedge between the two gardens as cover. I've felt for some time that someone's been watching from the hillside opposite, but never been quite sure.'

Ever since Stephanie had made the scene about how convenient it was, Holly had made a conscious effort to keep it bolted most of the time. She knew that the bolt had been on that night, she remembered doing it, and realised that Stephanie had probably been going to visit Duncan uninvited, otherwise he would have taken the alarm off first.

'From now on you are free to come and go as you please,' she grinned. 'My house is your house.'

'You don't care what the neighbours think then?' he joked.

'I trust my neighbours implicitly,' she replied. 'Not every one has such devious, not to say malicious minds as someone I could mention.'

Despite many attempts she couldn't elicit any more information from him. He mentioned that there weren't many places around Struan where strangers are accepted as normal, but that was all. She told him about the motor cruiser she had seen, saying it looked frightfully expensive to be owned by a local person, exactly the sort of boat a drug baron would need!

'I didn't say anything about drug

barons, young lady. Don't you go getting any ideas about detective work. I only thought to tell you about it since I don't want you placed in any danger because of my activity. I do wish you would reconsider and return to Prescot for a while. I hoped after your experience with Metcalfe you might be more amenable.'

She pulled a face. 'Peter apologised for his behaviour and sent me a lovely bouquet of flowers. He says he's leaving Struan at Christmas anyway. He merely misconstrued my friendship.'

'Huh,' he growled. 'You're not fit to be let loose. You need a keeper, or a ball and chain. Promise me you'll be on your guard, Holly.' He pulled her into the shelter of his arms and gazed into her eyes, looking deeply troubled. 'Please, sweetheart, I don't know what I'd do if anything happened to you. You are rather special to me.'

She didn't know what to say, being held in his vice-like grip was such a wonderful experience that she felt as if she had stopped breathing. She smiled invitingly up at him, willing him to declare that he loved her. He obviously had some warm feelings for her, shown by his concern. She was conscious of her own heart beating erratically.

His eyes were deep, disturbing pools, hypnotising her so that she couldn't think of anything but her love for him. By now she had accepted that she truly loved him and would do anything he asked, except leave Struan. She couldn't bear the thought of going back to Prescot and never seeing him again. That was asking too much.

His mouth descended and she responded eagerly to his invasion. At first it was a gentle teasing kiss which merely brushed her lips. Then Duncan gave a deep throated groan and she found herself clutched in his embrace, and was being kissed with intense fervour. It was a truly earth shaking experience as she was crushed against his firm body and she sensed his urgent, passionate response. It was something she had craved for so long.

Her hands found their way involuntarily round his neck as she clung to him. The fact that he was married no longer mattered, she wanted to belong to him. His kisses swamped her of all her senses. She wanted to please him and love him, she didn't care what anyone else thought. It was so wonderful being with him. A warm glow spread throughout her body, making it tinglingly alive from top to toe. She was transported into a dream world of delightful make-belief — a world where there was only the two of them and they belonged to each other.

'Holly, love. I'm sorry. I don't know what came over me. We'd best be going.' He set them apart and whistled for Shep.

Holly tried to recover her composure, feeling so shaken by what had happened that she literally trembled. Her face felt hot and feverish and she didn't dare look at him for fear of what he might think. He sounded so calm. Was she reading more into his kisses than she should? She really ought to stop dreaming and face reality. He wasn't the dashing, romantic hero from the latest novel she was reading. He was flesh and blood and not free to marry her.

'Come along, we'd better go find somewhere to eat. Are you hungry?' he asked looking at his watch. 'I hadn't realised how late it is.' Taking her hand they walked back towards the car. 'I'm not doing too well looking after you I'm afraid. Heaven knows what Cassie would think!'

Holly stumbled along the track, hardly daring to think. He must know how she felt about him now and he was obviously embarrassed. He had a quiet, restrained air about him. His kisses had taken her so much by surprise that she had responded automatically. She had never been kissed like that before and he hadn't been exactly unwilling! Was she being naive in thinking they meant more than he cared to admit?

They found a pub for lunch and during the meal Duncan asked her where she had met Alistair and what she knew about him, obviously trying to find a safe subject to talk about.

'He doesn't come to Struan much apparently, his main business is in Ireland. He's only here for a short holiday, and for the party which is to celebrate the Hunters wedding anniversary he told me.'

'By the way,' he said as their food arrived. 'I can take you there next Saturday, as I've been invited too.'

'By Ms Chloe Hunter-Johnson?' she asked archly.

'Hmm. She finally persuaded me. Since I knew you were going I decided to accept.'

Holly toyed with her cutlery, delighted at the news. 'Alistair was going to pick me up.'

'I'll ring and let him know that you have transport. That way we both have a good excuse for leaving early if we want.'

There didn't seem to be any reason not to go along with his suggestion, and in view of what had happened on their walk she was delighted to be going with Duncan. She couldn't understand her own feelings. She knew she shouldn't enjoy his company so much and that she ought to refuse his invitations, but she couldn't. Now that he was going to be at the Hunter's party she was looking forward to it.

After lunch they had another short walk to look at some waterfalls nearby but she noticed that Duncan remained quietly pensive for most of the time, and when they returned to the cottages he ruefully told her that he ought to get back to some work.

'So had I,' she said. 'Thank you for a lovely time, I have enjoyed it. I'll open the garage doors for you, shall I?'

She kissed him lightly on the cheek and hopped out of the car quickly. Her face was burning — she wanted to savour the time when he had held her in his arms, she could still remember how it felt when he had kissed her. It was something she would never forget, and even now when she thought how silly she was being, she didn't regret it. It was something she would always treasure, no matter what happened in the future.

As soon as she had opened the garage doors she hurried to her own cottage before he had time to see to Shep and lock up.

★ ★ ★

Nothing exciting happened during the next week. Holly began to wonder if Duncan had been trying to get her to abandon the cottage, because he wanted it all to himself and it had all been a fairy story cooked up for her benefit. It did sound so outrageous that anything like that could possibly be happening in Struan, and yet why had he kissed her and called her his love? Did he still think of her in a brotherly way? It hadn't seemed like a brotherly kiss as far as she was concerned! He had sounded concerned about her too, and not because he'd promised her aunt. Maybe, she thought, he was falling in love with her and knew how impossible the situation was. Maybe that was why he wanted her to leave.

The weather was cold and damp for most of the time, and though she scoured the loch with binoculars, she saw nothing at all suspicious. Holly was decidedly at a loose end. The painting wasn't going as she had expected, nor had the book project made much progress. She had cleaned the house from top to bottom and done a batch of baking. Moodily she moped about the sitting room wondering what to do next, when her eye fell on the photograph album.

Thinking that might yield some interesting snapshots of her childhood, she started flicking through it. Most of the photos were of people Holly had never seen before — very old fashioned judging by their clothing and austere faces. Then she came to some of herself, taken on her summer holiday visits, paddling in the loch or feeding the chickens, and chasing the old goat her aunt had owned at one time. She smiled as she remembered how it had eaten her best skirt right off the washing line.

Nothing much of particular interest there, but in an envelope, separate from the rest she found a faded picture of a handsome fellow cradling what she took to be a baby swathed in a huge shawl. One couldn't see much of the baby for the shawl, only a tiny screwed up face. She stared hard at the man in the photo, as if she had seen a likeness somewhere before. No, she muttered I must be imagining things, she couldn't place him.

Turning it over, she found on the back in her aunt's spidery writing the name Gordon and a date — now almost illegible. So that was Gordon — the man who had broken her aunt's heart! Holly looked again at the face of the man holding his son — why she smiled grimly, he had a look of Duncan about him. That's what she had seen. She must remember to show it him, it should amuse him. Her chance came the next evening when Duncan called to see her.

'I know this sounds corny, but do you think you could spare me a drop of milk?'

Holly laughed. 'Sure. No problem. Have you been so busy that you let the cow run dry?'

'I knocked the bottle over and spilt it,' Duncan confessed ruefully.

'Fancy a coffee?' she asked. 'I've got something I want to show you while you're here.' She produced the photograph for him to look at while she went to make the coffee.

'Does he remind you of anyone?' she asked re-entering the sitting room with the tray. She had expected him to be amused, but instead he looked embarrassed.

'I guess I have some more explaining to do. I should have thought to clear out Cassie's drawers.'

'Why?' she asked, looking puzzled. She motioned him to take a seat and offered him one of her home-made cookies.

'That,' he said, tapping the photograph. 'That is a photograph of my grandfather. You obviously saw the likeness.'

'But . . . but that is a picture of my aunt's lover by all accounts.' Holly stared questioningly at Duncan. 'And you say he is your grandfather? I don't get it. I didn't associate that Gordon with your cousin.'

'You are quite correct in thinking that he was your aunt's *gentleman friend* is how Cassie described him. Let me start at the beginning. Gordon — my grandfather had a son Iain and a daughter Janette — my mother. Iain and his wife were killed in a tragic car crash a few years ago. They were survived by their son, Gordon — named after his grandfather. He was the cousin I told you about. Grandfather doted on his son and grandson.

'I never got to know Gordon very well. He was younger than me and much more intellectual. He studied languages and philosophy and I heard he was a whiz on the piano. Anyway, you can imagine how heart-broken grandfather was when Gordon died as the result of the overdose, especially as he'd recently lost his own son. He lacked the will to go on living. Before he died, grandfather wrote asking me to visit him. I very nearly didn't go because of the shabby way he had treated my mother, but in the end I thought better of it. He was old and had no-one.

'When I met him, I felt terribly sorry for the old melancholy man, all alone in a gloomy house with only a dour housekeeper and his memories. I stayed for hours listening to his ramblings, trying to understand why I had been summoned to his presence after so many years. I knew of course that I was his last remaining close relative, but I didn't think he wished to acknowledge me, having turned against my mother like he had.

'Grandfather talked about Cassie at great length. His eyes misted over when he mentioned her, Holly. He really did love her, and bitterly regretted not being able to marry her. He told me how they met one day by the loch when grandma had gone to look after a sick relative. Grandma spent a lot of time over the next few months away from home, so grandfather, being lonely, had been befriended by Cassie.

'They used to walk and talk, and enjoy each others company, all innocent like, but when grandma found out she put a stop to it. Grandfather felt he couldn't do more than provide Cassie with a home of her own, so he gave her this cottage to live in as a sort of recompense for the pleasure she had given him. He was of the old school and would never even contemplate divorce.'

Holly by now was staring wide-eyed as the story unfolded.

'That was when he told me about these cottages and suggested I move in next door to Cassie so that I could keep an eye on her in her old age. Since my catastrophic liaison with Alison and her brother I was more than glad to take up his offer of the cottage. I needed a change of scene, so I moved in next door. I was glad to get away from Oban and its unhappy memories.

'I must say at first I was rather diffident about the undertaking to keep an eye on Cassie, but I soon learned what a wonderful person she was, and we got on famously. She was really no trouble.'

Duncan fell silent, reflecting pensively.

'All this happened about two years or so ago then I take it?' Holly remarked.

'Yes, about that. I gather you stayed with Cassie that Summer but I was away at the time, so I missed meeting you. Cassie was always talking so animatedly about you — always making excuses for you when a letter didn't arrive, or you didn't pay her a visit. She was lonely I know, but she was proud too and I felt so sorry for her, that I tried to make up for your apparent lack of concern for her well-being.'

Holly bit her lip with regret. 'I know, I feel bad about not coming more often. I didn't realise — the time just went. I know it's no excuse . . . '

'She did understand, Holly. I'm not blaming you. I know how it is when you're young and life is busy and full. Cassie realised that too, but it annoyed me when you turned up so promptly after her death, and you got full benefit of my caustic tongue. I was unbearable wasn't I?'

Holly smiled, secretly thinking about how she had likened him to a big, cuddly bear once in her thoughts.

'Cassie told me she wished you to have the cottage, because you dreamed of becoming an artist. She believed you could do it too. She had great faith in you.

'I'd heard how you'd spent your childhood holidays at Struan, and how you always wanted to stay when the time came for you to leave, so I went along with her request, thinking that you would soon find it unappealing after all. I couldn't see a city girl wanting to settle out here in the back of beyond; I didn't anticipate any problem, especially since you hadn't been for such a long time. I guessed you had changed, once you'd left school and started work. I thought it had probably been a childish fantasy and it had lost its appeal.'

'I've always liked Struan,' Holly said slowly, letting the implications sink in. 'Ever since I came as a little girl I've loved being here, and it has never lost its appeal in my eyes. I still adore it, but latterly I became immersed in my job and friends in Prescot, so the time seems to have passed by without my realising it. It came as quite a shock when I realised it had been two years since I'd paid a visit.'

'It happens,' said Duncan understandingly. 'You could say that our first meeting wasn't exactly auspicious. As I told you before, I think, you look remarkably like Alison from a distance, so I wasn't exactly enamoured of seeing you in more ways than one. Anyway, that is all water under the bridge now, I hope.'

'Did your grandfather come to see Cassie then — recently I mean?'

'No. I'm afraid he couldn't bring himself to do that. Cassie tumbled on to who I was — or rather mistook me for my cousin Gordon, but we hit it off extremely well. She was a great old lady. I reported back to grandfather once, shortly before he died. He seemed relieved to hear that Cassie was well and bore him no ill will. He was rather a sensitive individual under his dictatorial guise I discovered.'

'Poor, aunt Cassie,' said Holly sadly. 'I never really knew her at all. After all these years, I never suspected that she had a lover, never mind a child!'

'I didn't know she had a child.' Duncan looked startled. 'What happened?'

'He died apparently, at three months old — he was Gordon's child — the child in the photograph. I found letters from Gordon — warm, love letters. I read them, then I burned them.'

'The mystery deepens, as the saying goes.' Duncan got up to leave. 'I'm sorry if this is all unwelcome news to you, but since you noticed the resemblance, I didn't want you brooding over it. I hope I've cleared up some of the mystery for you. I'm still very glad you came, Holly, and you're welcome to stay as long as you like. I quite like having you as my neighbour. By the way, I hope you remembered to stock up your store cupboard, because it looks as if it might snow before long — maybe tonight even.'

8

The startling discovery had Holly at sixes and sevens. She realised that she hadn't seen any deeds for the cottage, but assumed the solicitor held them. Now however, it struck her that she shouldn't have inherited it at all. It wasn't Cassie's to give! From what Duncan had said, the property must all belong to him as the last surviving relative of Gordon. That was what he meant when he said that he didn't envisage any problem from a city girl. He hadn't expected her to stay, and since Malcolm Andrews did say that she couldn't sell the cottage, it was obvious that Duncan owned it.

There was a subtle change in the weather and overnight it snowed as Duncan predicted. The next morning Holly pondered her future, looking out at the Christmas card scene from her bedroom window. During the night she had firmly resolved to return home to Prescot, to seek advice from her father. She didn't feel she could put it in writing, she would have to see him personally and try to explain her true feelings. She knew her father would give her impartial advice if she asked for it, although she knew in her heart of hearts that there was only one answer to her problems.

She wished now that she hadn't arranged to go to the cocktail party because it meant she couldn't set off until Sunday morning at the earliest, but she couldn't duck out now, it might make Duncan suspicious. Besides which, it would be the last time she would be with him, so she didn't want to miss out on that.

Despondently she began packing her case, not relishing the long journey, but knew she had to do something positive. The situation couldn't be allowed to continue like it was. Sooty lay sprawled on the bed, washing himself lethargically as she hunted through the drawers for things to pack. She shoo-ed him out of the way irritably. I must remember to leave a note for Duncan to feed him, she thought sadly. She wished she could take him with her because he had been such good company and her confidante, but it was out of the question, at least on this trip.

'Sorry, old boy,' she called after him as he slunk out of the door. 'Next time, when I come back. I'll take you next time, I promise.'

Next time, she thought may be the last — in all probability it would be and she would have to arrange for Sooty to stay with her parents for a while, or maybe Roger. She could see herself returning to collect the rest of her belongings, and say good-bye to Struan and Duncan McCall for good. She stared round the room blinking away the tears at the very thought of leaving permanently.

Well, maybe it is for the best after all she thought. Her career as an artist hadn't been an overwhelming success, and she had become increasingly friendly with a married man, so maybe it's time to call a halt while I'm still in control. Was she still in control of her feelings she asked herself? She very much doubted it. If Duncan told her he loved her and asked her to stay she would do so without a second's thought.

All day Saturday she tried to find reasons for staying, but couldn't think of a valid one. At seven thirty she was ready waiting when Duncan called. This time she wore a peach silk shift with small cap sleeves and scalloped neckline — a dress she had bought for the Benson's Christmas dance the previous year and had only worn the once so Duncan hadn't seen it. Throwing a warm shawl round her shoulders at the last moment, she picked up her bag when he appeared and tried to summon up a friendly greeting.

Duncan smiled his appreciation.

'Well if that doesn't knock him dead then he wants his eyes testing.'

Holly grinned at his compliment and dipped into a curtsey. 'Thank you, kind sir.'

If only he knew that it had been him that she'd had in mind when she was getting ready and not Alistair. She wouldn't care if Alistair wasn't at the party, as long as Duncan was by her side. Indeed, she didn't want to share him with anyone else tonight, and would much prefer to spend their last evening together at the cottage quietly by the fireside. She was going to miss him so much. He was always in her thoughts. That was the trouble.

She wished she knew what went on behind those deep, thoughtful eyes. Indeed, what he thought about her. Her heart turned tipple-tails at the sight of him in his smart evening dress. He looked magnificent. She felt sure that he would be the most handsome man at the party. He would be in her eyes anyway.

'It rather looks like we're in for quite a fall of snow, which is most unusual this early in the Winter,' Duncan said, manfully controlling the car as it slithered along the lane.

'It does look lovely though doesn't it, floating in the headlights like feathers from a pillow fight.' Holly gazed childlike at the snowflakes.

Duncan grinned across at her infantile description. 'I hope you still feel the same when you have to walk back from the village in your high heels.'

'Oh! I should have brought my boots if it's going to get that bad.'

'Not to worry. I'm sure we'll make it, and I don't think wellington boots would go with that outfit! If it comes to a pinch I could always give you a pick-a-back.'

He could as well she thought, and she welcome it.

The party was in full swing by the sound of it when they arrived. Alistair and Chloe were obviously on the look out for them, they were both waiting in the hall and greeted them effusively. Holly and Duncan were introduced to Mr & Mrs Hunter and then were immediately taken in hand. Holly wished she could have stayed with Duncan, but Alistair whisked her away proprietorially. Chloe clearly wanted Duncan to herself as she led him off laughing gaily in the opposite direction.

'I'm disappointed not being allowed to come for you, little pixie,' Alistair censured her. 'I was looking forward to collecting you and perhaps taking our time getting here.'

Holly thought she ought to appease him. She smiled sweetly. 'Duncan thought it made more sense since we were both coming, to come together.'

'Sense maybe but not to my liking. Do you have to go back with him?' Alistair growled irritably and pinched her hand.

'I have arranged to,' Holly said beginning to feel uncomfortable by the possessive way Alistair was behaving.

She allowed him to escort her round the assembled gathering, his arm round her waist. She didn't wish to make a scene but didn't care for his disposition.

She smiled and chatted politely to the guests, all the while keeping an eye on where Duncan was. Even though it hurt to see him and to be with him she still wanted to spend as much time as she had left with him. The thought that soon she would be leaving Struan for good and would probably never see him again made her thoroughly miserable. She hoped that he would decide to leave early like he had intimated and they could possibly have a cosy hour or two alone.

She kept thinking about the trip home the next day, and hoped the weather wasn't going to prevent her from going. Now that she'd decided to leave she didn't want the snow to stop her. She had decided on positive action and she didn't want to be snowed in. She knew her resolve would probably weaken if that happened, she was already having second thoughts.

Most of the guests were elderly business men and their wives, obviously friends of Alistair's parents whose wedding anniversary they were celebrating. She sympathised with Alistair. It was all rather dull, with few guests of her own age. It was quite a large gathering, and she was thinking that she didn't recognise many people there when she suddenly spotted Stephanie. She was decorously hanging on to an adoring man's arm and flirting outrageously.

'Hello, Stephanie,' she greeted her sociably. 'Is Roger here with you?'

Stephanie giggled. 'No, Roger wouldn't come, more's the pity. It's a great party. I'm staying as Chloe's house guest. Isn't this a super place?'

'It certainly is, what I have seen of it,' replied Holly, who was feeling a little overawed and out of place. The atmosphere was too stuffy, with everyone remarking inanely on the weather, or the stock market, or what a mess the government was making of things. She was beginning to wonder why she had been persuaded to come in the first place. It wasn't her scene at all, and she rather doubted if Duncan was enjoying it either. She also felt uneasy with the way Alistair was holding her so conscientiously. She had tried to inch away from him, but that had only succeeded in him holding her still more firmly.

'Come, little pixie, now we have done the rounds I've done my duty. Let's make the most of the time we have together. I'll show you something of the rest of the house. Maybe I can change your mind about letting me see you home.' Alistair procured a bottle from a nearby table and a couple of glasses. 'Let me show you my etchings,' he grinned wolfishly, and grabbing Holly by the hand pulled her from the room and along a corridor, not giving her a chance to desist.

Holly looked round desperately for Duncan as she was dragged away, but he was nowhere to be seen. Alistair flung open a door of a dimly lit room pulled her inside and immediately slammed the door shut triumphantly. The noise of the door closing scared Holly and she quickly glanced round to see if the room was occupied. Unfortunately nobody else had found their way there.

It appeared to be a library. A log fire burned in the grate and two of the walls of the room were crammed full of books, row upon row from floor to ceiling, while the far wall had two large, heavily curtained french windows. A standard reading lamp was the only lighting, casting a dull glow on the leather upholstered furniture.

It was quite a pleasant room and Holly noticed the snow melting against the window panes as she wandered round now that he had set her free. She wondered how she could escape, the solid oak door had shut out all sound of the party. Memories of Peter Metcalfe sprang to mind and she shuddered inwardly. How did she get herself into these situations?

'Oh, Holly, thank goodness you've come to save me from all those horrors out there. You can see why I don't come home very often. I don't think I could have survived another minute amongst such bores.' Alistair came up behind her and pulled her down on to the settee. He poured out the wine and handed her a glass.

'To us, my dear. Drink up, the night's still young. We've got oodles of time. This is more like it. You are my salvation. You know that don't you?'

Holly by this time was totally bemused. 'I don't see any etchings,' she remarked jokingly, but glanced anxiously at the closed door. She was wondering if Duncan had seen her being hustled away. If he had would he realise that it was against her will? Would he come to her rescue if she found herself out of her depth again? At least there were lots of people not too far away, she ought to be safe enough she thought.

'Here's to you, my little pixie.'

Alistair's closeness was quite intimidating, and she wondered how much he'd had to drink already. Holly sipped her wine cautiously, but found it quite pleasing.

'Hmm, that's nice and sweet. Just as I like it.'

'And so are you, darling.'

Alistair disposed of his glass and immediately she was entangled in his arms. His hands seemed to be everywhere. Then his mouth claimed hers before she had chance to object. She was somewhat at a disadvantage because she was still holding her glass and she didn't want to spill the wine on the carpet. Finally she managed to put it down, but then she found her arms trapped by his as he pushed her back against the cushions. He was lying on top of her and all the time smothering her with kisses. She wanted to scream but couldn't as he ravaged her lips.

When he paused to adjust his hold on

her she managed to gulp breathlessly. 'Please, Alistair. Let me up.'

'Oh, my little spitfire. You look so inviting. The moment I first saw you I knew that you were meant for me. Don't look so offended, my darling, you must feel it too. You've been enticing me in a most desirable way. What big, beautiful, bewitching eyes you have, my dear. Such gorgeous, sensuous eyes that a man could drown in. I can't believe you are as innocent as you pretend to be. Not with your — equipment,' he snickered.

'Please, Alistair. I thought we were supposed to be at a party. We should go and join the other guests. Duncan will be looking for me.'

'Why should he?' he said, all surly. 'You came as my guest. He's not you gaoler is he?'

'No, of course not. Please let me up. You're spoiling my dress.'

'You'll have to ask nicer than that.'

It was as if he had turned into a different person. He wasn't at all like she had believed him to be. When they had gone to dine at the Castle he had behaved with utmost courtesy. Now he was like a wild maniac. His face was flushed and he loosened his tie, protesting that it was rather warm.

'What happens if I undo this zip?' He murmured teasingly inching the fastening of her dress down a little way. 'Maybe it would be better to take your dress off, if you are bothered about creasing it.'

Holly screamed near to panic.

'The doors in this house are extremely thick so no one will hear you. Besides, I have ways of keeping you quiet,' he laughed menacingly.

Before she could scream his mouth covered hers with brutal, savage kisses again and though she writhed and squirmed violently she couldn't escape. She was passing out with fear as she felt his hands sliding down the top of her dress when the door of the library opened and she was relieved to hear voices. Thank goodness there hadn't been a key to lock the door she thought.

'I'm sure I saw her come in here.'

It was Duncan, and sounding none too pleased. She felt so relieved.

'Isn't that her over there in the little black number,' Chloe said irritably. 'Let's have another look amongst the guests in the lounge. I'm convinced she wouldn't have come in here.'

'No, that's Stephanie, I'm looking for Holly and she's in apricot. She was heading this way when I last saw her, I'm positive.'

While this discourse was going on Alistair got to his feet swearing viciously under his breath. Holly struggled to sit up, vainly trying to tidy herself. He'd been watching out for her again, thank goodness!

'Ah, there you are, Holly. I'm afraid we'll have to leave a little earlier than we intended, my dear. It rather looks as if the snow is coming down sufficiently heavily for the road to be blocked before long, and you are not exactly dressed for hiking through snow drifts remember.'

He looked across the dimly lit room, but only his steely eyes gave away the anger he obviously felt. Holly went red with embarrassment under his grim scrutiny, his eyes flicking icily to glare at Alistair.

Chloe stood in the doorway glowering at her brother. 'Dad's been looking everywhere for you, Alistair. You've been neglecting the guests. You'd better go and make your peace with him.'

Alistair stood like a statue in front of the fire, his hands stuck deep in his pockets, then with an angry retort strode out of the door, nearly knocking over the reading lamp as he weaved to avoid Duncan.

Scowling malevolently at Holly, Chloe quickly followed her brother from the room without another word.

Once they left, peace descended on the room. Only the crackle of the logs on the fire, and the rhythmic ticking of a clock on the mantelpiece could be heard.

'Are you all right, Holly?' Duncan approached the settee and sat down next to her. His voice now gentle and soothing. 'Did I interrupt at an untimely moment?'

'Oh, no.' She collapsed into his arms and sobbed. 'I'm so glad to see you. What is the matter with me? What do I do wrong? Why do they all think like they do?'

Duncan held her in his arms, rocking her gently until she calmed down. 'Hush, my love. I'm here now. They don't know you like I do. They don't look any further than your beauty and open friendliness. You have too trusting a nature, I'm afraid.'

'I'm sorry, I always seem to be crying on your shoulder. I don't mean to.'

He smiled tenderly, wiping her eyes with his thumbs. 'I've got broad shoulders, and I can't say that I mind comforting you. You are a very desirable young lady, as I'm sure all the fellas around here will agree. You are infectiously friendly.'

'I only want to be friends not ravaged the minute we are alone,' she sobbed.

'I know. Come along, let's head back home before the lane gets blocked.' He helped her with her zip, and waited while she freshened up her make-up. 'Do you feel up to saying our good-byes, or would you rather we sneaked out through the window?' he asked.

'I'm all right now thanks. As long as you are with me, I think I can cope.' She smiled her gratitude. 'You're the one person I can trust it seems, apart from cousin Roger.'

'Don't be so sure of that even,' he grimaced. 'You can turn any man's head, Holly. I'm not immune, I do assure you.'

The snow was certainly building up they found as they motored home but it was wet slushy snow which left the roads reasonably clear.

'Did you come away from the party early because of me?' she asked in a subdued voice once they got under way. 'The snow doesn't look to be a problem.'

'It was a good excuse, and I rather thought you were ready to leave. That sort of do isn't my cup of tea.'

He was watching the road, but Holly sensed his mind was on other things.

'Have I caused you a problem then?'

'No, my dear. In a way you have helped. I wanted to see who attended the Hunter's party, and you provided an excuse for our leaving early. Did you by any chance recognise anyone there?'

'Not many. Stephanie of course, and Malcolm Andrews the solicitor, but otherwise only some familiar local faces that I can't put names to. Why? Are the Hunters involved in the drugs ring?'

'Did you see any strangers — not locals?' he asked.

'One or two people I didn't recognise at all so they could be strangers hereabouts, I wouldn't know. What's going on Duncan?'

'Well, it seems as if drugs appear soon after the Hunter's have a get together. There is obviously a tie in somewhere.'

Holly shivered and Duncan squeezed her hand. 'Nearly home and there will be no need for you to walk the length of the lane after all.'

Leaving the car outside on the roadside he ushered Holly into his cottage.

'I think you'll be safer here tonight. I'll leave the alarm on and Shep will keep you company, but I'm afraid I have to go out again. I must first make a phone call though. How about making us some coffee while I change?'

Holly was full of questions she wanted to ask but she could see he was eager to be away, so she did as he suggested and made the coffee. The questions she wanted to ask were irrelevant anyway. Struan was not going to be her home for much longer. She couldn't go on like this, torturing herself and embarrassing Duncan.

When he returned a few minutes later having changed into a dark sweater and jeans, he quickly drank the coffee she'd made. 'I hope not to be too long, but you'll be all right, won't you? Don't answer the door to anyone.'

'Yes. I'm fine, honestly,' she said, hanging her head sorrowfully.

He pulled her into his arms and tipped her chin up so that she had to look at him. 'Holly, when I get back we must talk you and I. OK? We can't go on like this.' Then he gently kissed her. 'Don't cry, sweetheart. I'll look after you. I promised Cassie I would, didn't I? I'll try to be as quick as I can.'

She heard the sound of his car manoeuvring as she despondently rinsed out the beakers in the kitchen. It was no use, she would have to go before she made a fool of herself completely. Tears ran down her face as she walked through the connecting door and up the stairs to collect her suitcase.

She couldn't bear to wait for his return only to be told that he loved her, but that he was already married and couldn't get a divorce for some reason. Somehow she guessed that was what he meant and she knew how honourable he was. She must have made it plain to him exactly how she felt and she was ashamed. Ashamed and humiliated by her own weakness. She was making the task set by aunt Cassie almost impossible for him to carry out.

She changed into a warm jumper and slacks then scribbled a note for Duncan, leaving it on the kitchen table along with a painting she had done of Shep, which she had been going to give him for Christmas. After making sure the alarm was set she threw her case on the back seat of the car and set off for Prescot. She hadn't time to pack the rest of her belongings, but maybe Roger would come for them if she asked him nicely.

She hadn't driven much in snowy conditions before and with the mood she was in she was somewhat anxious, but she was determined to be far away from Struan before Duncan returned. She wouldn't embarrass him any more with her stupidity. She would get out of his way — out of his life forever. It was the best for all concerned.

Driving passed Hunters Moon she saw the festivities were still continuing, lights shone from most of the windows and music could be heard even at that distance. She wondered if Duncan had returned there after taking her home, and whether Alistair was mixed up in the drug racket — or Chloe even. So much for nothing ever happening in Struan! Whatever would her parents think?

Once clear of the houses the road meandered for a while before joining a major road, and from then on it would be reasonable travelling conditions. Having once passed Hunters Moon she slowed down and let her thoughts wander on to what Duncan would do when he found her missing. Would he come after her? Would he be pleased that she had now done as he wanted her to do in the first place? Would she ever see him again? The last brought tears to her eyes again. Maybe the best thing would be for her to go and visit Cousin Tracy in Canada for a while, until she had hopefully got over her foolishness.

How she managed to avoid him she would never know. Slamming on the brakes she slithered to a stop with her heart in her mouth. The figure had appeared from out of nowhere. She wound down the window, letting in an icy blast of cold air which helped clear her brain.

'Are you all right?' she enquired as the man collected himself up from the hedge and approached the car.

'Why, thank goodness it's you, Holly. What luck.'

'Malcolm! What on earth are you doing out here?'

'Can you give me a lift?' he said brushing snow off his clothes. 'My car's broken down back there.'

'Sure. Hop in.'

He squeezed himself into the passenger seat and rubbed his hands together. 'My but it's cold out there. I was wondering how long I'd have to wait for a lift.'

'What happened? You must be perished without a coat.'

'The car refused to start. Probably the battery I suppose. I'm not mechanically minded. I'll have to get the garage to see to it on Monday. I should have gone back inside and rung for a taxi, but didn't want to disturb the party.'

'Where were you heading?' she asked engaging first gear.

'Back home. Would you mind? It's only round the far side of the loch.'

Holly nodded. 'Just give me directions.'

He fiddled with the seat belt as she set off again and shortly he directed her along a minor road which skirted the loch and soon they were pulling up outside some impressive looking gates.

'There's no need to go down the drive. I can walk the rest. Thanks very much for coming to my rescue. I'd ask you in but unfortunately the house is empty and I wouldn't want to impugn your reputation.'

She grinned. 'That's all right. I'd best be on my way. I'm going back to Prescot.'

'Safe trip,' he replied quite casually. He sounded pre-occupied and not at all like his usual self Holly thought as he set off down the drive at a brisk pace before she had even turned the car round.

Travelling conditions were quite tricky so by the time Holly arrived at the junction of the motorway she thought it advisable to call a halt. She pulled into a motel which fortunately still had a vacancy and slumped down on the bed dejectedly. She didn't want to arrive in Prescot in the early hours of the morning anyway and have to get her parents out of bed. She knew she would have some explaining to do when she arrived and she needed time to think first about what she was going to tell them.

9

'Hello, Mum. Got a spare room?' Holly asked brightly, sounding much more lively than she felt. The journey had seemed like an eternity. She'd hardly slept a wink at the motel. She felt so sad and disillusioned, thinking about what a mess she'd made of everything. She'd set off for Prescot very early, still undecided what she should tell her parents.

Once en route she was glad that she had stopped though, as the radio reported there had been a spate of accidents due to the poor road conditions. She passed many abandoned vehicles on the roadside, several in need of a tow truck by the look of them.

'Holly love. What are you doing here, not that it isn't nice to see you. Nothing wrong I hope?'

'It's a long story. I'd better tell you

and Dad both together.'

'Dump your case in room 202 then. It's free for the moment. We'll have coffee in our sitting room and you can bring us up to date. Have you had any breakfast? You're looking a little peaky. Not sickening for something, I hope?'

'I'm OK, Mum. Back in a minute.'

When Holly slipped into their private sitting room a short time later, her father had also arrived and looked anxiously at her.

'Are you all right, Holly? Your mother says you have problems. You're certainly not looking too good.'

'Not exactly problems, as one big problem,' Holly said ruefully. 'My next door neighbour, to be exact.' She decided to come right out with it and tell them everything. 'I've learned that aunt Cassie didn't actually own the cottage, so it wasn't hers to leave to me. In truth it belongs to Duncan McCall, my neighbour. I've only just found out.'

'How come?' her father asked. 'How

did you find that out now? I don't understand. Surely — '

'Did you know about aunt Cassie and a man called Gordon?'

Her parents looked bewildered and shook their heads.

'Well,' said Holly. 'Apparently, a long time ago, aunt Cassie was in love with this man Gordon and even had a child by him. However, it appears he was already married, so he bought the cottage for aunt Cassie to live in. Anyway, the baby died and Gordon went back to his wife.'

Her parents stared at her in total disbelief.

'It's true. Every word of it. I found some letters that this man wrote to aunt Cassie, and some photographs too. Anyway, Duncan McCall — my next door neighbour happens to be Gordon's grandson would you believe!'

'So you've decided to let this man McCall have it, even though Cassie wanted you to have it. Is it all legal?' her mother asked. 'Maybe you ought to get some professional advice, love. It all seems — '

'It doesn't matter one way or the other,' Holly interrupted. Tears sprang to her eyes as she continued, deciding to get it all off her chest once and for all. She chewed hard on her bottom lip in an effort not to cry.

'Duncan said I could stay — that I could have the cottage because Cassie wanted me to have it, but I find that I can't do that either, because I . . . I fell in love with him, and he's already married.' She broke down. She sobbed, 'It's all such a shambles that I decided to come home. I thought I'd pay a visit to cousin Tracy for a while, to give me time to think. I'm sorry to come — '

'Holly love, what can we say. You do need time to sort yourself out. Don't go rushing off until you've calmed down.'

'No, I won't, Dad,' she promised, dabbing away the tears. 'I don't want to be a nuisance. I know you're busy. I didn't know what to do. I thought

I'd spend Christmas in Canada.'

'What does this next door neighbour have to say for himself? Does he love you? Is he getting divorced?' her mother asked, putting her arms consolingly round her daughter's shoulders.

'I don't honestly know, Mum. I . . . we didn't discuss it. I got so confused, I felt I had to leave to save him any embarrassment.'

'At least, now you'll be here for your birthday, won't you?' her father said in an effort to cheer her up. 'Then, if you want to spend Christmas with Tracy we'll understand. That seems like a very good idea of yours. Tracy would love to see you I am sure, and you'll be able to meet your nephew at long last.'

Holly sniffed. 'Struan isn't the quiet place you think it is, you know. You'd be amazed at what goes on that sleepy little village.'

★ ★ ★

After lunch Holly went for a walk. She had half hoped that Duncan would have rung, even though as far as she knew, he didn't know where to find her. He was never far from her thoughts despite her best efforts otherwise. She couldn't help but wonder what he'd thought when he returned to the cottage and found her gone.

The snow hadn't persisted as far south as Prescot, but it was cold and raw out, so she soon returned to the hotel and settled in her room out of the way. She tried to read but couldn't concentrate. Then she listened to the radio but it couldn't drown out her unhappy thoughts. Finally, she rang Roger on the pretext of returning the books he had lent her.

'Holly, what are you doing in Prescot? When did you get back?'

'Just this morning. If you're not doing anything, can I come round and return those books? I'm a bit at a loose end.'

'Of course. I'll be delighted to see

you. I'd offer to come over there, but I guess here is more private. Come and pour your heart out to Uncle Roger.'

She might have known that Roger wouldn't be taken in. She knew she could rely on him to understand. When she arrived at his flat half an hour later, he ushered her into the warmth and poured her out a generous glass of wine.

'Now then, what's the trouble? What are you doing down here, Holly? It's Duncan McCall isn't it?'

'How did you guess?' she asked with astonishment.

'My dear girl, it stuck out a mile that you're in love with the fellow. I hope Steve's shenanigans didn't upset the apple cart! I could strangle her sometimes.'

'No,' she sighed. 'It's not Stephanie's fault. It's Duncan, he's married.'

'Oh gosh. I am sorry, Holly. Are you sure?'

'Well, he didn't say it in so many words . . .' She shrugged her shoulders.

'I am surprised. He didn't look the sort to lead a girl on like that.'

'He hasn't led me on at all. He's behaved in a most circumspect way at all times — like a big brother in fact. Take last night, when we went to a party at Hunters Moon — we saw Stephanie there by the way. Alistair Hunter was getting a bit fresh with me, until Duncan intervened. He's been keeping a friendly eye on me because he promised aunt Cassie he would. No, it's all my own fault, I know.'

'I suppose Steve was in her element at the party,' Roger remarked bitterly. 'She wanted me to go with her, but I didn't take to the Hunters the last time we met. They looked like the nouveau riche — a bit too superficial for my taste. Maybe I was plain jealous — I don't know.'

'I can't say they give me any joy. I hope Stephanie knows what she's doing, because Duncan thinks the Hunters are in some way involved with drugs.'

'That doesn't surprise me, but Steve's a big girl and can look after herself. It might even teach her a lesson if she gets rounded up as one of them.' He grinned vindictively. 'Come on, let's finish the bottle. We can both do with cheering up.'

'Sorry, but I'm driving.'

'Well, you'll jolly well have to get a taxi home then, won't you? Shall we eat in or out?'

Roger was a marvellous sinecure. They ended up concocting a meal together, and watched a film on television. He was one person she felt she could be herself with and relax completely.

It was much later that she set off for home.

'Thanks, Roger. I feel so much better now. Maybe it's the wine or maybe it's being with you, but whatever — I am grateful.'

'You've always been my favourite cousin.' He smiled as he helped her into the taxi. 'You never know, things usually work out in the end, given time. Chin up, old girl.'

'I hope they work out between you and Stephanie too.'

'She's got some growing up to do first, I reckon,' came the reply.

★ ★ ★

All the next day Holly tried forlornly to keep herself occupied. She busied herself about the hotel, helping her parents in any way she could, but every time the phone rang her heart lurched in anticipation of it being Duncan. She didn't know whether she wanted to hear from him or not. She vacillated between longing for him to ring just to hear his voice, and yet not wanting to be disillusioned at the thought that he did love her, but could not marry her. At one stage she wished she'd stayed at the cottage to hear his story, but in truth she didn't want it confirmed.

Later that night as she prepared for bed, she was in tears — miserably lamenting the fact that he hadn't rung. Only one more day, she said sadly to herself. I'll give him one more day. What a fine way to spend a birthday!

The next afternoon Holly sat surrounded by clothes. She was desperately trying to pack, but her heart wasn't in it. She gazed miserably at herself in the dressing table mirror and her lack-lustre eyes stared back from her pale gaunt face. The strain of trying to maintain a calm exterior in front of her parents was beginning to tell, she looked decidedly ill.

Pull yourself together, she berated herself. This won't do! Didn't you make a pact with yourself that you'd put him out of your mind once and for all? Obviously he's not for you. He'd have been in touch by now if he thought anything about you. Stop deceiving yourself. We've been over and over all this. You're going to stay with Tracy. You have things to do.

Taking up her blusher, she smoothed some on her cheeks in an effort to disguise her pallor. That's better, she muttered. Tomorrow I'll be on the plane, and maybe I can begin a new life in Canada with a bit of luck. Now to finish packing, and get ready to meet Roger.

'Holly.' Her mother entered the bedroom. She looked worried thought Holly, but that was not unusual. Something in the tone of her voice though made Holly frown anxiously.

'Nearly packed,' she said. 'Did you want something? I can easily finish this later.'

'Roger's downstairs.'

'He's early.' Holly said, glancing at her watch. 'I thought we'd arranged for seven o'clock.'

'He's . . . he has some news for you. Shall I ask him to come up?'

Holly froze. She knew instantly that it must be bad news. She could tell from the way her mother was looking at her — or rather not looking at her. She couldn't look her in the eyes. What little colour she did have, now drained from Holly's face. Slumping down on to the bed she whispered, 'Please, Mum.'

In no time at all Roger appeared. He sat down on the bed beside her and put a comforting arm round her shoulders.

'It's Duncan, isn't it?' she mumbled hoarsely. She felt faint.

'Hmm. He's in hospital, I'm afraid.'

She started. 'Oh no! What happened? Where is he?' Her breathing came in great gasps.

'It appears he was involved in a motoring accident. I don't know all the details, but he's still in one piece.'

'He's going to be all right?'

From his hesitant manner she knew there was something else — something he hadn't told her.

'What is it? What's wrong? Roger, please tell me. Is he going to be all right?' She was beside herself with concern.

'As I said, Holly, I don't know all the details, but I gather he's concussed.

Look, I know we were supposed to be going out tonight celebrating, but in the circumstances I thought . . . '

'I must go to him.' Holly was on her feet immediately.

'What about your flight? I thought you were . . . '

'That can wait,' she snapped. 'Come on, we're wasting valuable time. Are you coming with me or do I go on my own? Where is he?'

'Of course I'll take you. Calm down, love. It won't do Duncan any good you arriving in a state.'

'Sorry,' she said, already half out of the door. 'How did you come to hear about the accident?'

She urged him down the stairs, desperate to get under way.

'It was a pure fluke actually. I was chatting on the phone to a sales rep I'd met in Edinburgh and Duncan's name cropped up. The chap said how sorry he was when he'd heard about the accident. Apparently he lives near Kirkston and the motorway pile-up was reported on the local radio. It happened near a place called Little Craven I gather.'

It took them nearly two hours to get to the hospital. The clock outside said almost eight o'clock when Roger pulled into the car park. Nothing much had been said throughout the journey. Holly was too keyed up to chat, she felt all knotted up inside. She kept wondering why Duncan was on the motorway. Had he been on his way to see her? Maybe he was going to see his wife? Was it somehow connected with the drugs business? Round and round her thoughts went, half hoping, half afraid.

'I'd better come in with you, Holly. You are OK, aren't you?'

She merely nodded. Now that they had arrived she was wondering if she was doing the right thing. What if Duncan wasn't alone? What if . . . ? Somehow, her legs propelled her through the swing doors, passed reception and down umpteen miles of what seemed like endless corridors. She was certainly glad of Roger's support — his hold on her arm was rock steady.

Eventually they came to the room where they'd been informed Mr McCall was. Her heart was in her mouth as they pushed open the door. It was a private room with the one bed and the blinds half drawn. Stepping cautiously inside she walked over to the bed to the sleeping figure of Duncan. She gasped at the sight of him, his head swathed in bandages. He looked so pale — so deathly white. Then, without thinking she bent to kiss him lightly on the cheek.

'Hello, Duncan,' she whispered, catching her breath as he stirred and sighed.

The sound of Roger greeting someone, startled her. She spun round to face another occupant of the room. He'd been sitting in a chair in the corner, but now stood at the bottom of the bed watching intently as Duncan moaned.

'You wouldn't be Holly, would you?'

he asked softly. His voice was the gentle Scottish burr so similar to Duncan's.

She nodded, afraid to speak for fear of bursting into tears. The sight of Duncan lying like that really upset her. Roger answered for her, introducing them both. The man looked so like an older version of Duncan that she knew instinctively that he was his father.

'How is he?' Roger asked.

'They say he's comfortable!' the man growled.

'What happened?' Holly finally found her voice. 'What's the matter with him?'

'My son was on his way south by all accounts, when he was involved in a multiple car pile-up. They say there's not a lot wrong with him — mostly superficial bruising, but he just lies there, not recognising even me. He keeps calling for someone called Holly.' He turned to look her. 'I thought at first he meant a tree — maybe he'd hit one, but then he muttered about promising Cassie something. Then I tumbled to the fact that Holly was a person.'

There was an awkward pause when no one spoke, then they all turned towards the bed when Duncan called out again for Holly. She went to his side immediately, and bent to kiss and reassure him. The sight of him lying there so helpless made her tremble. She wished and wished that he would open his eyes and get better. She felt certain it was all her fault that he was there at all. Oh, why had she left Struan like she had? Why hadn't she waited for his return? If she had this would never have happened.

Suddenly his eyes flashed open, at first with a blank, vacant expression. Then, with a startled cry he sat up and hugged her. 'Holly? Are you all right?' he asked.

She didn't know whether to laugh or cry — he was worried about her! She didn't know what to say so she hugged him back, so relieved by his normalcy.

Next Duncan became aware of the others in the room and seemed a little shocked when he realised where he was. 'What happened?' he asked them. 'Where on earth am I? Why am I here?'

They all started talking at once, trying to fill him in.

'I could do with a cuppa,' remarked his father with a wide grin. 'They don't allow anything stronger around here, I suppose.'

'I'll join you, if I may?' Roger said with gallant diplomacy.

When the two men left the room, Holly bit her lip nervously.

'Are you all right, Holly?' Duncan asked again. 'You look awfully pale.'

'I'm fine.' She sat down on the chair by the bedside, relieved and anxious at the same time. 'You had me worried though.'

'I remember now,' he said slowly as his memory gradually came back. 'I was on my way to see you. I was upset when I returned home and found your polite little note. I thought we were going to talk when I got back.'

'I thought I'd save you any more embarrassment,' she said quietly, twiddling her handkerchief into knots.

'Why should I be embarrassed? I would have taken it on the chin if you'd told me that you wanted nothing more to do with me, never fear, but I would have preferred you to tell me in person. Is that what you had in mind, Holly?' He took hold of her hand and squeezed it.

'No,' she whispered, her heart was pounding and her breathing erratic. 'No, Duncan, it wasn't that. Only — '

'Well then, why did you run away? Have I — '

Fortunately for Holly, a nurse arrived at that judicious moment, quickly followed by a doctor and they asked her politely to leave.

'Don't go far,' Duncan ordered, releasing her hand very reluctantly. 'We haven't finished our conversation.'

After promising to return, Holly

went out into the corridor where she found Roger and his father waiting. They procured a seat for her and some lukewarm coffee in a plastic cup. Duncan's father smiled at her benevolently.

'I have a lot to thank you for, young lady. It was like a miracle seeing him come alive like that. Just the sound of your voice was sufficient. He obviously thinks a lot about you, my dear.'

'He promised my aunt that he'd look out for me when I went to live next door,' Holly said. She felt awkward and shy — it was a tricky situation. 'I'm glad that he appears to be on the mend.'

'Another twenty-four hours and Holly would have been on her way to Canada,' Roger remarked. 'We were about to go out to celebrate Holly's birthday when I heard what had happened.'

Duncan's father scratched his head. 'I was beginning to think that you must be Duncan's girl friend?'

Clearly he was puzzled, so Roger tried to clarify the situation for him. 'Holly is my cousin. Her aunt Cassie bequeathed her the cottage next door to Duncan's. When Holly went to live there your son kept a brotherly eye out for her.' Catching her eye he went on. 'Unfortunately, Holly learned something which caused her to flee back home.'

'Not this damn nonsense to do with drugs?' Mr McCall remarked. 'I wish he'd never promised the old fool he'd co-operate. Leave it to the professionals I say.'

There was another lull in the conversation as Roger looked at Holly for inspiration.

'Has anybody got in touch with his wife?' Holly asked quietly.

'Who's wife?' Mr McCall asked.

'Duncan's,' Roger answered quickly, realising how much courage it had taken for Holly to even make the suggestion.

'He hasn't got a wife that I know

about.' Duncan's father replied drily. 'Kept it rather quiet if he has.'

Roger took Holly's hand in his and squeezed it hard. 'I heard that he married someone a few years back — Alison somebody or other wasn't it?' he said innocently.

'Huh. Thank God he didn't marry her. Her and her no good brother caused more than enough grief to last a lifetime.' Duncan's father had wandered over to the window to look out, unaware of the shock that his news had given Holly. 'Duncan swore he'd never marry after that disaster — that was why I couldn't understand him calling for you, young lady. After that Alison woman he vowed he'd remain a bachelor for the rest of his natural life, and have nothing more to do with women, period.'

Holly sat hardly daring to believe what she was hearing. He wasn't married! Duncan wasn't married! It pounded in her brain like a hail shower. She felt Roger nudge her.

'Are you all right, Holly? You're not going to pass out or anything are you?'

'No,' she stammered, before she slithered gracefully to the floor.

To Holly the remainder of the evening was a complete blur. She had vague impressions of worried faces and being offered a glass of water, then being carried out to the car. But where was she? Her sleepy eyes refused to focus. The room was only small and unfamiliar.

'Good morning, sleepy head.' She heard Roger's voice as if in a dream. 'Sorry to wake you, Holly, but I have to get moving. I've got work I must do.'

Eventually Holly prised open her eyes. 'Gosh, Roger, where am I?'

'In the Red Lion. Jim and I brought you here last night. Don't you remember?'

'Who's Jim?' Holly asked in alarm.

'Jim McCall — Duncan's father — you remember him surely?'

'Oh, yes, of course.' Holly gradually

gathered her wits. 'What time is it?'

'Nearly seven. Jim said he'd look after you, but I have to be on my way. You don't mind do you?'

'No, that's all right, Roger. I'm a bit dim-witted this morning.'

'That's no surprise. You'll be all right when you've made your peace with Duncan.'

Holly sighed. 'I didn't dream it all then?'

'You should have seen Duncan when he heard you'd fainted — he was ready to leap out of bed then and there. If that's not love than I don't know what is! The nurses had a hard job persuading him that you would be better after a good rest, and that went for him too. If I were you though I shouldn't wait too long before going to see him, or you might find him hiking down here in his pyjamas.' Roger grinned amicably. 'Look after yourself, Holly. I'm glad you're not going to Canada. I would have missed you.'

When Roger had gone, Holly lay back against the pillows with a smile on her face. The description of Duncan getting so worried about her made her heart leap. To think that if Roger hadn't learned of Duncan's accident she would be setting off for the airport! She found that sleep was now impossible, she was far too excited to stay in bed.

After a reviving shower she got dressed in her rumpled clothes and cautiously went downstairs. The Red Lion it appeared was only small, and she wondered what time they served breakfast because she was feeling decidedly hungry.

'There you are. How are you feeling this morning, young lady?' Jim McCall greeted her in the entrance having returned from an early morning walk round the village. 'You're looking a better colour this morning. Got some colour back in your cheeks.'

'I'm fine, thank you, Mr McCall. I'm sorry if I put you to a lot of trouble last night.'

'Not at all. The name's Jim by the way. Come along, let's see about some breakfast, you must be about famished. Your cousin has had to leave, I gather.'

'Yes, he had to get back to work.'

'You weren't thinking of running away again, were you?' Jim McCall asked somewhat sternly. 'Duncan would never forgive me if I turned up this morning without you. I've never seen him so agitated.'

'No,' replied Holly. 'I feel a little foolish, but . . .'

He patted her hand. 'Don't worry. I understand. Roger and I had quite a long chat last night after you turned in.'

Jim McCall was charming. He escorted Holly with gentlemanly courtesy, and he seemed as impatient as Holly to visit the hospital to see how his son was. He was a comforting sort of man — broad shouldered like Duncan, although not quite as tall. He had a gentleness about him which Holly found most endearing.

After a huge breakfast they set off, both eager to see how the patient was, and hoping that there had been no relapse overnight. They arrived soon after nine, and as they walked down the corridor outside Duncan's room they could hear an argument taking place.

'I want my clothes, dammit. I'm leaving I tell you. If you don't get them for me I'll walk out in these revolting pyjamas.'

'That's Duncan. He sounds on form,' remarked Jim with a wry grin.

As they entered Duncan's room they nearly collided with a red faced nurse who rushed out, muttering uncharitable words under her breath, something about *ungrateful patients*.

'Now then, son, that's no way to treat 'em.'

'Huh! Bossing me about like a two year old. I'm perfectly all right. I want to get out of here. I've work to do.'

With Jim's hand in the small of her

back Holly was propelled toward the bedside.

'This young lady has been under the mis-apprehension that you had taken yourself a wife,' his father said in a calm no-nonsense voice. 'I told her that it was news to me, but who knows what you've been up to that I don't know about. What with all this to-do with the Customs people and the Police. Perhaps you'd best clear up a few doubts in her mind while I take a walk eh, son. You'd best make it quick though because she's supposed to be flying to Canada today.'

Jim found a chair for Holly, and with a reassuring nod to his son strolled out of the room.

Holly sat on the edge of the seat nervously playing with her fingers. She didn't think her legs would support her, they seemed to have turned to jelly at the sight of Duncan again. She hadn't known how she was going to open the conversation, but his father had taken the wind out of her sails with his blunt announcement.

'Holly, is this true?' Duncan asked incredulously.

Holly gulped and nodded her head.

'Come here, Holly.' He patted the bed. 'I want to hold you. Oh, confound those nurses. Where are my damned clothes? I'm getting out of here right now. This is no place for what I want to talk to you about.' He was about to ring the bell when the same nurse bustled back carrying his clothes over her arm. She looked none too pleased.

Duncan growled his thanks. 'Tell Dad, I'll be five minutes, Holly will you? And don't you do any disappearing act,' he added grimly, already throwing back the covers. 'I'll follow you to Canada if I have to. We have some unfinished business.'

He sounded so wonderfully masterful. She couldn't wait to have the position clarified — she loved him desperately, and it rather looked as if the feeling was reciprocated.

Fifteen minutes later they were in Jim's car heading for the motorway. The staff had all tried to persuade him otherwise, but Duncan remained obstinate, he was determined to go home. He said he felt fine and promised to take it easy for a day or two, but he wouldn't stay another minute. Holly was full of questions but understood Duncan's need for some privacy. She was so relieved by the way things were turning out that she felt she could wait until they were alone. It was all going to work out fine — she knew it.

'What happened about the drugs episode, Duncan?' she asked eventually. 'I gather from your father that it had a successful outcome.'

'Well, your good friend Malcolm Andrews won't be available for a few years all being well. He was caught red-handed.'

'Malcolm! Good heavens,' she exclaimed.

'Didn't you wonder at his extravagant lifestyle? I couldn't see how he supported that large house, boat and a spendthrift wife all on a small town solicitor's income?'

'I didn't know him very well,' Holly said. 'I only met him a couple of times in Kirkston, except for the night of the party. I gave him a lift to his house that night after I nearly ran him down. He said his car wouldn't go. I never liked him very much, he was too smarmy for my taste. So what happened?'

'The weather played its part this time in his downfall. Luck was on our side for a change. Usually when the Hunters had a shindig Andrews would go across in his boat apparently, but this time he had to use his car because of the blizzard-like conditions. The customs men sabotaged his car, but somehow he still managed to evade them. Obviously you unwittingly aided him to escape.'

'Gosh. I didn't do it on purpose. They won't blame me will they?'

'No. He got wind that something was amiss and made a run for it. He's been under suspicion for some time but there was no evidence against him. Then, after you dropped him off, he gambled on the weather and took his boat out, but fortunately by then the customs men had already realised he'd given them the slip. They waylaid him before he got far out to sea.'

'Was that why you went to the party then? As a sort of spy in the camp?'

'Partly,' he replied, giving her a hug. 'First and foremost though I was jealous of Hunter, and since I didn't trust him an inch where you were concerned I wanted to see that no harm came to you. I persuaded Chloe to invite me, although she seemed a little reluctant which surprised me. She's been chasing me long enough.

'Also, if drugs were being circulated I didn't want you involved. I wasn't sure what to expect and couldn't warn you beforehand. The fewer people in the know the better. I don't suppose you would have heeded my warning knowing you. You would have been all the more keen to go. Anyway the customs people said it would be advantageous if I could verify if certain individuals were present at the party and let them know.'

'I would have thought a large gathering such as that would be the last place anyone would choose to pass on a consignment.'

'Hmm. That's what I thought too, but apparently the conspirators don't trust each other and prefer to be amongst a crowd of people when they make the exchange. After all it wouldn't need to be particularly bulky. We aren't talking about huge hauls you know.'

'Who else was involved then?' Holly asked.

'The Hunters are all squabbling amongst themselves I gather. They're all disclaiming any knowledge of the drugs. My guess is that it's down to Chloe. I can't for the life of me see her parents getting involved, or Alistair come to that, even though I don't like the guy. I suspect Chloe set everything up — the parties, etc.

as a cover up. She certainly kept a keen eye on me the whole time we were there.

'The customs people were tipped off that the drugs were appearing locally soon after the Hunters had a party — that put them on to them in the first place. It was an unknown source who divulged that bit of information, but Chloe's ex-husband was chief suspect. Revenge I shouldn't wonder for the way she treated him in the past. He's been spotted in the neighbourhood recently — in his boat. At first he was a suspect too. He was one of the guys I spotted acting suspiciously that I told you about.'

'Gosh! And my mother says nothing ever happens in Struan!' Holly was stunned. Held close in Duncan's arms she watched the scenery flashing by. Ever since they'd left the hospital he hadn't let go of her — not that she wanted him to. She couldn't wait to be alone with him, to hear what he had to say. She liked his father very much but she couldn't wait for them to be on their own. She was pleased to see that Duncan looked so much better this morning, although the bandage round his head gave him a wounded soldier appearance.

As they approached Struan Holly suddenly remembered that there would be nobody at the cottages.

'What about Shep and Sooty? Who's taking care of them?'

'The farmer's looking after them,' Duncan informed her. 'I rang him before I left home and he promised to go down and feed them each day. I didn't anticipate being away so long though. When I got back that night and found you'd gone I set off immediately thinking I might overtake you en route. I was making good time too until I got tangled up in traffic on the motorway. Some damned fool travelling too fast for the conditions pushed me off the road, otherwise I was doing fine.'

'You must have past me then because I stopped for the night at the motel

287

before the motorway. I didn't fancy driving in the snow, and also I didn't want to wake my parents in the early hours either.'

He sighed. 'I never thought of that. I wasn't thinking too clearly, I guess. I wanted to catch you up. I had my heart in my mouth several times when I saw a red car off the road and relieved when I saw it wasn't yours.'

Jim drew up outside the garage. 'Here we are folks, home again. I'll only stop for a cuppa and then I'll have to be on my way.'

'We can fix you up with a bed for the night if you want, Dad.'

'No, son, thanks all the same, but I ought to be getting back. My *housekeeper* will be anxious about me. I'll love you and leave you to the tender mercies of this young lady. And since you haven't got transport you'll have to take things easy.' He winked at Holly.

'Isn't it time you married your

housekeeper, Dad, and made an honest woman of her?'

'You're a fine one to talk, son,' Jim McCall said with a good natured grin. 'Maybe you're right though.'

10

An hour later they bade Jim good-bye. Holly kissed him affectionately on the cheek and thanked him for his kindness in looking after her.

'Look after him, Holly,' he whispered. 'He's not as tough as he seems. Underneath he's unsure and vulnerable. You've knocked him for six you know.'

'I will, I promise,' she replied feeling a lump in her throat. 'I do love him.'

'What were you two whispering about?' Duncan quizzed as they walked back into the cottage.'

'I promised your Dad that I'd make you put your feet up,' she said in her best school ma'am tone. 'He's worried about you, as I am too. You should by rights still be in that hospital bed.'

'If you promise to keep me company I will take the weight off my feet,' he replied promptly. 'I do feel somewhat wafty all of a sudden.'

Immediately Holly became anxious and started plumping up the cushions on the settee, urging him to lie down and rest.

'Are you sure you're all right, Duncan? You should have stayed in hospital for at least another day to be on the safe side.'

'I shall be all right when I've had a chance to talk to you, Holly. Come here, I want no more interruptions. I've waited long enough.'

She went willingly into his arms and nestled against his chest with a contented sigh.

'Now then, I believe you have some explaining to do. What's all this about you thinking I was married? Where did you get that crazy notion from, may I ask?'

'Well . . . ' Holly didn't know what to say. She realised how stupid she had been for taking what Malcolm said as true, after all he had said it was only hearsay. 'Malcolm Andrews mentioned . . . '

'I might have known he'd be at the bottom of it,' Duncan exploded angrily. 'And you believed that villain? Holly, why on earth didn't you ask me? Now everything begins to make sense.'

He gave her a reassuring hug and a long passionate kiss. It was a little while before they continued the conversation.

'I know we didn't get off on the right foot when you first arrived, but I did think that after a while you were at least beginning to like me. Ever since that night we went to the Kings Arms I have been utterly captivated by you. You changed from a gangling teenager into a beautiful temptress before my very eyes. I couldn't get you out of my mind.

'I did try to act the big brother, hoping that in time you might find me a possible suitor. I didn't know how else to handle the delicate situation. Cassie had entrusted your safe keeping to me, but I hadn't bargained for you being such a seductive young woman.'

She grinned with amusement. 'Is that so?'

'I was quite plainly jealous of Roger until I learned he was your cousin. Then I wanted to punch Metcalfe to kingdom come for frightening you the way he did. You didn't seem to realise the danger you were in. And as for Hunter — I was beside myself with anger from the mauling he was giving you that night.

'I'd seen you looking anxious earlier, so I tried to keep you in sight, but it was rather difficult as there were so many people milling about. I didn't trust young Hunter. I had a feeling he wouldn't stay around too long mixing with the guests — they weren't his type, I surmised.

'At one stage I saw you talking to Stephanie, and then I lost sight of you. Then at the last minute I caught a glimpse of someone wearing peach disappearing along the corridor.

I guessed it was you. It took me a little while to fight my way through the crush, especially as Chloe seemed bent on delaying me.'

'Oh, Duncan. I'm so glad you came when you did. I was terrified.'

'I made up my mind then and there that I had to declare my feelings to you. I couldn't go on watching you get hurt. If necessary I was prepared to leave Struan. I couldn't stay around and see you going out with other men any more, despite my promise to Cassie. I didn't know what you felt for me — whether I was too old for you even.

'I had intended waiting until this drugs business was finished, thinking that you'd be safe then. My grandfather's house is still vacant, so I decided I would go there if you turned me down, but one way or another I had to know where I stood with you. I was obsessed with you to the point where my work was suffering. I couldn't concentrate.

'The meeting with the customs men

was already arranged unfortunately so I had to go, more's the pity. From what you said at the Hunters, and the way you behaved, I thought there was possibly a chance for me and I couldn't wait to get home.

'I returned as soon as I possibly could, and I was devastated to find your note. For a split second I thought I ought to leave well alone, but I could see that you'd been crying — the writing was all wavy and smudged. So without wasting any more time I jumped back in the car and set off after you. I guess you know the rest.'

'Oh, darling Duncan, I do love you. I've been trying my best not to fall in love with you, ever since Malcolm told me you were probably married. That was why I went out with Peter and Alistair — to try to get you out of my heart. I've been so miserable. I've always derided my friends when they've gone out with married men, but I was coming round to the conclusion that I'd even be your mistress if that was the only way I could be with you.'

'What have I done to deserve you, Holly? Will you marry me, sweetheart?'

'Oh yes, Duncan. Yes, please.'

She savoured his kisses. Delighting in the sense of warm security she felt in his arms.

'I gather that yesterday was your birthday, and today, at this very moment you should be winging your way to Canada. Will your cousins ever forgive me do you think? How can I make it up to you?'

'Tracy will understand — she's a romantic at heart, and of course Roger latched on to the fact that I was in love with you long ago, so he won't be at all surprised.'

'I'm sorry to have spoilt you birthday, Holly.'

'You gave me the best birthday present I could possibly have wished for.' Holly's eyes sparkled with tears of joy.

Duncan frowned. 'Holly, you aren't

thinking of me as a father figure, I hope?'

'I should hope not!' She looked startled. 'What are you getting at, Duncan? I don't understand.'

'Well, I know you have this habit of leaning on people — Roger in particular to help you make decisions — like a big brother, I suppose. I thought you might be thinking of me in the same light.' He paused before adding, 'I know I'm a good deal older than you, Holly, but I . . .'

'You can stop right there! I don't know whatever gave you the idea that I can't make up my own mind. With Roger, it's something that developed over the years. He likes to be thought of as my protector and all that. It bolsters his macho image, but I can make up my own mind when I need to. I stayed here didn't I? That was my choice, wasn't it?'

Duncan grinned back at her fervent denial. 'Ouch! OK. You win.' He kissed the tip of her nose. 'I'm glad to hear it. Although staying here was in truth Cassie's idea. Once she left you the cottage you felt that you ought to go along with her wishes, I suspect. You've been trying to fulfil an ambition to please her.'

'I suppose so,' Holly reflected.

'Anyway, I'm glad that you did decide to stay.'

'Even though you find me a trial?' she chuckled.

'You don't seem to realise the effect you have on the opposite sex, Holly. I certainly didn't care for the way Metcalfe and Hunter manhandled you, but I could understand it up to a point. You drive men wild with your endearing, artless, friendliness. You look so naive and guileless.'

'I suppose I ought to own up to being a complete innocent,' she whispered. 'I hope I won't disappoint you. I know in this day and age — '

'My love, I'm delighted to hear it. You could never disappoint me. I'm an old fashioned guy too don't forget.

Perhaps that was why Alison thought me boringly pedantic. I believe I told about Alison didn't I?'

They spent the rest of the day restfully planning their future together. They both agreed that the cottages would be a wonderful place to start married life, although Duncan remarked that he didn't think they would be big enough for the family he was hoping for.

'How many children had you in mind?' she giggled, digging him in the ribs.

'How about half a dozen to be going along with! I always fancied brothers and sisters to play with.'

'Me too,' she agreed. She would have agreed to anything. Just being in his arms was heaven after all her disconsolate thoughts back in Prescot.

By ten o'clock Duncan was yawning continuously.

'I promised your father I'd make sure you had an early night in bed,' Holly said sternly. 'Are you going to go quietly? You'd have been tucked up ages ago in hospital.'

She was quite surprised when he agreed without a murmur. He did look pale and tired, she thought, and hoped he wasn't having a relapse. The cottages were rather isolated and they didn't have any transport. She wondered where the nearest doctor lived in case of an emergency.

She watched him climb the stairs rather lethargically, and pondered what she should do. She hadn't got a bed made up in her own cottage because she hadn't wanted to leave him for a minute since they'd returned home.

She went round making sure the doors were all locked, the alarm set and the animals comfortably settled. Then she rinsed out the coffee beakers and thought how wonderful it was being back in Struan and in Duncan's cottage. She was so thankful that she wasn't flying off to Canada, never to see Duncan again. At that very moment she should have been meeting her cousin Tracy.

Finally she tip-toed up the stairs. She was feeling a little nervous, but she knew that she wouldn't sleep if she went to her own lonely bed. She did contemplate bedding down on the settee, but felt she needed to be where she could keep a watchful eye on Duncan — he still worried her. Ever since she'd first seen him in the hospital bed she'd felt guilty, and now he'd discharged himself early because of her. She knew his father was rightfully worried — concussion was not to be taken lightly.

She rather expected Duncan would be asleep by now because he had looked tired, so quietly she entered the bedroom, grateful that he had already turned out the light. The room was bathed in ghostly moonlight, which at least made it light enough to see by. Quickly she slipped off her clothes and was about to creep into bed when Duncan spoke softly.

'You look quite ethereal, darling. I'm

301

not sure this is a good idea. I'm only human you know.'

'I promised your father I'd take care of you,' she stammered. 'I'd worry all night if I wasn't here. Besides which my bed isn't made up.' She knew she was making excuses.

'That's as maybe, but . . . '

'I don't have a night-dress — I left without even an overnight bag, I was in such a hurry.' She was glad of the darkness which covered her blushes.

'I'd offer you my pyjama jacket only I don't happen to be wearing one.' She heard the chuckle starting. 'Come here, sweetheart the suspense is killing me.'

Holly dived under the covers and buried her head against his chest feeling thoroughly embarrassed.

The bed creaked as Duncan turned to draw her into his arms.

'I was hoping you'd come to me, Holly although I didn't feel I should suggest it in the circumstances. I too wouldn't sleep knowing you were worried. I'm fine. Truly I am. But you may as well get used to the idea that I am a very jealous man as well as being an impatient one. I want you so very much — I have done for what seems like an eternity.'

She sobbed with delight and hugged him as he kissed her tenderly and his hands soothingly caressed away her fears. She whimpered as he finally roused her to such a pitch that she shuddered with emotion, hearing his tender words of love through a veil of increasing need. The last thing she remembered before falling into a deep satisfying sleep, was Duncan mumbling that the sooner she wore a gold wedding band the better he'd like it.

The next few days were pure unadulterated happiness for Holly. She thought she ought to feel guilty but she didn't — she couldn't. Duncan loved her. They were going to get married as soon as it could be arranged and they would live happily ever after. It was sheer bliss.

They spent Christmas in Struan,

promising to visit with her parents when Duncan was fully recovered. Actually he was soon his usual self again but it was a good excuse for them to spend the time alone.

THE END

Other titles in the
Linford Romance Library

SAVAGE PARADISE
Sheila Belshaw

For four years, Diana Hamilton had dreamed of returning to Luangwa Valley in Zambia. Now she was back — and, after a close encounter with a rhino — was receiving a lecture from a tall, khaki-clad man on the dangers of going into the bush alone!

PAST BETRAYALS
Giulia Gray

As soon as Jon realized that Julia had fallen in love with him, he broke off their relationship and returned to work in the Middle East. When Jon's best friend, Danny, proposed a marriage of friendship, Julia accepted. Then Jon returned and Julia discovered her love for him remained unchanged.

PRETTY MAIDS ALL IN A ROW
Rose Meadows

The six beautiful daughters of George III of England dreamt of handsome princes coming to claim them, but the King always found some excuse to reject proposals of marriage. This is the story of what befell the Princesses as they began to seek lovers at their father's court, leaving behind rumours of secret marriages and illegitimate children.

THE GOLDEN GIRL
Paula Lindsay

Sarah had everything — wealth, social background, great beauty and magnetic charm. Her heart was ruled by love and compassion for the less fortunate in life. Yet, when one man's happiness was at stake, she failed him — and herself.

A DREAM OF HER OWN
Barbara Best
A stranger gently kisses Sarah Danbury at her Betrothal Ball. Little does she realise that she is to meet this mysterious man again in very different circumstances.

HOSTAGE OF LOVE
Nara Lake
From the moment pretty Emma Tregear, the only child of a Van Diemen's Land magnate, met Philip Despard, she was desperately in love. Unfortunately, handsome Philip was a convict on parole.

THE ROAD TO BENDOUR
Joyce Eaglestone
Mary Mackenzie had lived a sheltered life on the family farm in Scotland. When she took a job in the city she was soon in a romantic maze from which only she could find the way out.

NEW BEGINNINGS
Ann Jennings

On the plane to his new job in a hospital in Turkey, Felix asked Harriet to put their engagement on hold, as Philippe Krir, the Director of Bodrum hospital, refused to hire 'attached' people. But, without an engagement ring, what possible excuse did Harriet have for holding Philippe at bay?

THE CAPTAIN'S LADY
Rachelle Edwards

1820: When Lianne Vernon becomes governess at Elswick Manor, she finds her young pupil is given to strange imaginings and that her employer, Captain Gideon Lang, is the most enigmatic man she has ever encountered. Soon Lianne begins to fear for her pupil's safety.

THE VAUGHAN PRIDE
Margaret Miles

As the new owner of Southwood Manor, Laura Vaughan discovers that she's even more poverty stricken than before. She also finds that her neighbour, the handsome Marius Kerr, is a little too close for comfort.

HONEY-POT
Mira Stables

Lovely, well-born, well-dowered, Russet Ingram drew all men to her. Yet here she was, a prisoner of the one man immune to her graces — accused of frivolously tampering with his young ward's romance!

DREAM OF LOVE
Helen McCabe

When there is a break-in at the art gallery she runs, Jade can't believe that Corin Bossinney is a trickster, or that she'd fallen for the oldest trick in the book . . .

FOR LOVE OF OLIVER
Diney Delancey

When Oliver Scott buys her family home, Carly retains the stable block from which she runs her riding school. But she soon discovers Oliver is not an easy neighbour to have. Then Carly is presented with a new challenge, one she must face for love of Oliver.

THE SECRET OF MONKS' HOUSE
Rachelle Edwards

Soon after her arrival at Monks' House, Lilith had been told that it was haunted by a monk, and she had laughed. Of greater interest was their neighbour, the mysterious Fabian Delamaye. Was he truly as debauched as rumour told, and what was the truth about his wife's death?

THE SPANISH HOUSE
Nancy John

Lynn couldn't help falling in love with the arrogant Brett Sackville. But Brett refused to believe that she felt nothing for his half-brother, Rafael. Lynn knew that the cruel game Brett made her play to protect Rafael's heart could end only by breaking hers.

PROUD SURGEON
Lynne Collins

Calder Savage, the new Senior Surgical Officer at St. Antony's Hospital, had really lived up to his name, venting a savage irony on anyone who fell foul of him. But when he gave Staff Nurse Honor Portland a lift home, she was surprised to find what an interesting man he was.

A PARTNER FOR PENNY
Pamela Forest

Penny had grown up with Christopher Lloyd and saw in him the older brother she'd never had. She was dismayed when he was arrogantly confident that she should not trust her new business colleague, Gerald Hart. She opposed Chris by setting out to win Gerald as a partner both in love and business.

SURGEON ASHORE
Ann Jennings

Luke Roderick, the new Consultant Surgeon for Accident and Emergency, couldn't understand why Staff Nurse Naomi Selbourne refused to apply for the vacant post of Sister. Naomi wasn't about to tell him that she moonlighted as a waitress in order to support her small nephew, Toby.